KILL SHOT

A BRIAN KILBRAIDE THRILLER

DON SIMKOVICH
LON CASLER BIXBY

CARVED IN STONE MEDIA
WWW.CARVEDINSTONE.MEDIA

This is a work of fiction. Names, characters, places, and incidents are products of the author(s)' imaginations or are used fictitiously and are not to be construed as real. Any resemblance to actual events, locales, organizations, or persons, living or dead, is entirely coincidental.

ISBN: 979-8-356265-94-5

Story based on characters created by Lon Casler Bixby for an original screenplay.

Cover Artist: Ben Southgate
Interior Book Design: Bob Houston eBook Formatting

Published by Carved in Stone Media
www.carvedinstone.media

ACKNOWLEDGMENTS

Special thanks to our Beta readers for their input, honesty—and finding the typos we missed:

Grace Harrell, Cyndie Santopietro, Lars Nilsson, and Trella McMaster-Snyder.

We're grateful for Ben Southgate and his fabulous cover design. He was able to create the art exactly as we had envisioned.

Behind the scenes we cannot forget to thank Bob Houston, who has done the e-book and print formatting for each of our books.

We also appreciate the encouragement and support of our family and friends, and in turn, we acknowledge and value those who put their lives on the line to help others.

***

CHAPTER ONE

Cars clogged the westbound lanes of the highway during the morning commute. The drivers moved slowly but steadily through the fog of Silicon Valley with brake lights blinking on and off. Thousands of motorists drove across an overpass just like they did every day, completely unaware of the world below where a man, surrounded by a swamp, was perched on a spit of dry ground a thousand yards away.

He wore an oversized parka that was baggy and torn. His shopping cart positioned near him was full of cans, glass jars, cardboard, and bits of rotting food in empty to-go boxes. His patch of land with his one-man dome tent had become his kingdom a few days earlier. Tall reeds separated him like a curtain from the shabby homeless encampment off cardboard shacks and torn canvas tents that were shrouded in the wispy clouds down a winding path.

The April chill would help him focus. He peered north through his rangefinder across the wetlands and used the overpass like a picture frame to give perspective. The traffic's steady hum of tires and engines slowing down and speeding up faded into white noise and helped him concentrate on the details of an office building that came into view.

In these final moments to prepare for his assignment, he pulled off the heavy coat and tossed it on the ground. He no longer looked like all the other homeless. A long-sleeved nylon shirt that swimmers used in cold water fit smoothly over his Black, muscular body.

The building was a few stories high. The walls were a cold mix of concrete and plenty of glass revealing steel girders and lots of open space inside. On top of the building was an A-frame tower made of clear glass like the spire of a cathedral.

Just enough sunlight was breaking through the fog to glisten off the building and welcome a stream of cars exiting the highway, passing near the visitor's lot, and moving single file in front of the building on the way to the company's sprawling parking structure.

Inside the A-frame was a glass-enclosed patio. The rangefinder was an amazing tool, magnifying the view. Even though the spot was just over 1,500 yards away he could see men and women wearing black slacks and white shirts, setting up trays of delicacies and plenty of coffee urns. The shareholder's meeting was about to get underway.

His phone vibrated in his jeans' pocket and he pulled it out to read a cryptic text message: *On schedule.*

A map with GPS showed two blue dots, the busses, blinking and moving slowly toward the building that was shown as a red teardrop on the map. The fog was gradually lifting as the temperature began to climb.

He stood, grabbed the shovel out of his shopping cart, and dug the dirt by his tent as a voice shouted cheerily, "Hey there, Grunt."

He turned to see a skinny man with a scraggly beard bobbing and weaving up an uneven path.

"Hey there, backatcha'." He had told the man earlier in the week that his name was Grunt. Everyone else ignored him since they thought he was just another hurting man passing through life, but the skinny guy liked to talk, especially when he was high, or needed something to get high.

"Dude, where'd you get that body?" The skinny guy laughed. "You pumping iron?"

Grunt wasn't amused. "Is there something you need?"

He looked around. "You got something to smoke?" A fly buzzed at the base of the man's beard, but he didn't notice.

"No, sure don't," said Grunt. *No time to talk.*

"Damn. I need a smoke or something." The man wore a beanie, scratched at his hairline, and eyed the grocery cart. "Hey, when you turning that shit in?"

"Don't matter, does it?" Grunt grinned. "You know why I like my spot here?"

"Why?"

"'Cause I got lots of privacy." His voice was crisp and clear.

The man eyed him up and down and looked hurt. "Yeah, okay. We all got reasons. I was just being friendly. Hey, there's a new recycling center opened up. The walk's a bitch, but I hear that they sure as hell is paying good."

Grunt's phone vibrated. The screen showed the blue dots were getting closer. "Guess what?"

"Chicken butt," the man laughed and tugged on his beard nervously.

Grunt didn't change his expression.

"Dude, you need to change your name to Grump."

"I got a lot on my mind. Here, take these." He dropped the shovel, picked up a garbage bag filled with glass jars and cans, and handed it off.

"You mean it?"

"Yeah." Grunt wanted to dig. "I ain't going nowhere today. My shoulder's stiff. Old injury."

"Okay." The man brightened up. "I'll bring you back some CBD to ease your pain."

Brakes squealing in the distance caught Grunt's attention. He turned. It was a delivery truck heading to the parking lot, but not the busses.

Grunt smiled. "Sure. Better go now. You want to beat the others."

The man scratched his side and smiled. Yeah, like I got a lot of get-up-and-go."

"That's right. So, get going."

The man waited and looked at Grunt's cart. Attached to the handle was a funny-looking gadget with a wing and a small fan blade. "What's that?"

"An anemometer."

"Huh? Say what?"

"A weathervane." Grunt grumbled this time and stared at the man with annoyance.

The skinny man looked like he was going to say something else, but then threw the sack of cans over his shoulder, turned, and walked away, bobbing and weaving down the path and through the swamp.

Grunt took the rangefinder, knelt behind the reeds, and studied the activity on the patio. The food was set on tables to the right. A podium was erected at the far wall. This is where the *Genius* would stand to speak. More men and women grabbed coffee and food. He could see a woman's necklace glistening. And there he was, the Genius himself. Taller than the others and wearing his trademark wire-rim glasses. He was only in his thirties and already one of the richest men in the world and in charge of the most influential social media network on the planet.

Along the glass wall, Grunt envisioned several different spots where the Genius would hopefully stand. He was ready. He set the rangefinder aside again, looked to see if anyone was coming up the

path. No one. At this time of the morning, most of the homeless were still sleeping it off or heading to the food bank.

Grunt grabbed the shovel, dug quickly, and uncovered a moisture-proof canvas gun bag. He opened it, reached inside, and pulled out a rubber bag that was totally dry. Inside were the components of a Barrett bolt-action MRAD-MK 22 sniper rifle with optics. He preferred the larger .50 caliber of the M82, but times were changing and this weapon with its new 338 Norma Magnum round would get the job done with precision.

The anemometer's wings were moving in the morning breeze and gave a reading on wind speed and direction.

Another look through the rangefinder showed the elite audience settling into chairs and the Genius acting relaxed and chatting near the podium.

Sounds of grinding engines filtered back under the overpass and across the swamp. Grunt looked. The busses had arrived. Protestors with signs, banners, and bullhorns stormed out toward the building's entrance, just below the glass patio. Grunt listened but couldn't hear anything more than an angry hum and what sounded like chants. The protestors would do their jobs, not even knowing why they were really there. Diversion—the oldest trick in the book.

The busses blocked the arriving cars, causing confusion. The meeting had just gotten started.

He quickly assembled the gun, attaching the sound suppressor to the end of the muzzle, and then the riflescope and bipod to the picatinny rail. He moved into position laying prone on the cold dirt and looked through the scope. He had constructed his encampment as a sniper's hide to shoot from.

The crowd of protestors swarmed around the building's entrance while others looked up to the patio, shouting and raising their fists. And then it happened. The Genius left the podium and started moving to the glass wall overlooking the chaos below. He stopped, laughed, and after observing for a moment stepped back from the window.

I got all day. Grunt calmed his breathing and found that inner rhythm that was so necessary for his work as a professional. *Do what you need to do, Mr. Genius.* The target moved back toward the podium, and as if on cue, the crowd grew into a frenzy.

Suddenly, the Genius changed directions and headed back to the glass wall. The woman in the necklace joined him and so did another man. The trio shook their heads in amusement at the commotion below.

The Genius stepped forward, leaned against the glass to get a better look, and that's when Grunt pulled the trigger. The gun shot with a bang and *whoosh*, but the noise quickly faded and within two seconds the bullet exploded through the glass wall and into the Genius' face, right between his eyes. His wire-rim glasses split perfectly in two. A red mist filled the void where his head had been. Skull fragments and gray matter covered the attendees as chaos erupted.

Grunt took a calming breath. He pulled the bolt back, ejected the cartridge, and pocketed the spent round. He methodically broke down the weapon and packed it and the rest of the gear inside the bags. There was one more thing to do.

He unzipped a pocket of the gun bag and pulled out a pen and specially made patch. He scribbled a name across the back and left it inside the flap of the tent. He slipped into his parka, slung the packs over his shoulder, and walked down the path. He quietly hummed as he made his way over the soggy ground, passing a homeless man standing and peeing outside his cardboard shack.

"Howdy," said the man who finished and pulled up his zipper.

Grunt gave a little salute, walked on, and pulled out his phone. He sent a one-word text: *Done.*

CHAPTER TWO

It was bad enough that he didn't have time to shave after waking up late, but lukewarm coffee wasn't how Detective Tom Stone wanted to start his day. He took another sip from his mug and then poured it into the sink. Having something hot and steaming sounded comforting before going into the morning briefing.

"Not to your liking?" asked his partner Jake, making his way into the breakroom and turning his wide shoulders to the counter.

"It's not hot."

Jake stuck his cup in the microwave and hit the timer. "Make a note. New coffee pot needed."

Stone sniffed the air and stepped away from the microwave. "That stinks. Who cooked fish in that? Make note. Need new microwave."

"Some things never change," mused Jake, a Black man and former running back in college and the NFL. "Back in college before a big game, we had this third-string quarterback who was always cooking up ramen with fish and stunk up the whole locker room. That smell is still stuck in my sinuses." Jake glanced at his phone. "Hey, meeting's about to start. You coming?"

"Yeah, I'll be in." Stone picked up a file folder off the counter and started rifling through the pages of notes inside.

"You know, it's much easier if you come into this century and just scroll a tablet. Same info but it's neatly organized at your fingertips."

"I prefer the old-fashioned way," said Stone.

The timer dinged and Jake pulled out his cup. "You finding anything unusual about the case?"

"I hate to say just another San Fernando Valley shooting, but—nothing too descriptive."

Jake sipped his coffee. "That's too bad."

Stone watched. "How does it taste?"

"Hmm, not very good. Kind of like fish sauce." Jake made a face as he hurried out. "See you in a minute."

Stone gave up on fresh hot coffee, poured another lukewarm mug, stuck it in the microwave, hit the timer, and reflected on his notes. A man who was walking near an underpass along the Los Angeles River was shot. No eyewitnesses came forward and they were checking into the victim's background.

The microwave dinged, Stone pulled out his mug and spilled a spot of coffee on his white dress shirt. "Damn."

Jake stormed back into the breakroom. "Stone, come on."

"I'm coming, I'm coming." Stone tried to sip from the mug but burned his lip on the rim. "Damn."

"Stone?"

He set the mug on the counter. "Yeah, what's the rush?"

"No, up north." Jake was worked up. "It's unbelievable."

"What?"

"Captain Harrell heard about it. A shooting at ProfileScene.com. It sounds like Julius Brae was shot and killed."

"You're kidding. Julius Brae? The tech genius himself? Really? When?"

"This morning. Just a little while ago." Jake dashed out and Stone followed him into the conference room. Captain Harrell was sitting glued to his laptop, monitoring info from departments around the Bay Area.

"Sit down," said Harrell. Kyung Harrell had the tough outer layer of his father, a Marine who was stationed in Korea where he met and married his mother.

Stone and Jake settled at the table with the other detectives.

"So damn strange." Harrell eyed his laptop.

"What happened?" asked Stone.

"Julius Brae was gunned down. The shareholders meeting on the company's main campus was just getting started when protestors showed up. Sounds like Brae stepped to the window to look out and was shot dead."

Murmurs of shock and surprise rolled around the room. Harrell eyed his monitor as reports were streaming in. "Others being treated."

"Multiple dead?" asked Jake.

"Can't tell. Looks more like others wounded. Flying glass," said Harrell. He looked at Jake and Stone. "Christ. That's going to send ripples."

"Yeah, sure will." Jake was thoughtful. "Someone builds a company like that. Hundreds of millions of users worldwide. Hard to believe."

"It sure is," said Stone.

Brian Kilbraide, an athletic Black man and one of the younger detectives, walked in and sat down. "Good morning. Damn, streets getting all dug up around Hollywood. Thought I'd never get here."

"I was wondering," said Jake. "We almost sent a search party. You hear the news?"

"What?"

"ProfileScene. Julius Brae was murdered at their headquarters."

Kilbraide looked stunned. "Really? Oh, my God!"

"I wonder what my girls will say," mused Stone. "That's their connection to life."

"Seems like half the world's connection to life," said Jake.

"Wow. Any leads? Any ideas who did it?" Kilbraide settled into his chair. He pulled out his phone and started scrolling for information. "Guy like that. So smart."

Captain Harrell set his laptop aside: "No, too soon. Info's just coming in. San Jose PD's going to have their hands full. I don't envy them. But in the meantime, we have our own cases to solve. Alright gentlemen, time to get to work. Stone, what's the latest on that underpass shooting yesterday?"

Stone spread a printout in front of him. "Victim taken down near Riverside Drive and the 170 Freeway. Got an approximate time of day when it happened. But that's about it."

Jake agreed. "I've been canvassing the area and there's nothing. Been to the bars nearby, thinking a fight or argument spilled out into the streets. No one saw or heard anything."

Kilbraide looked up from his cell in surprise. "Captain Harrell, excuse me but, ProfileScene just went down. Completely offline."

CHAPTER THREE

Bob Stevens logged off his phone, reading coverage from around the globe on Julius Brae's death. It was now twenty-four hours since the killing and every news outlet from the Bay Area to the BBC in the U.K. and throughout Asia kept probing, digging through angles, and reporting on every detail. Nothing was insignificant. The media went on to speculate that the outage at ProfileScene was due to hackers from Russia and North Korea and the company was working hard to get the site back online.

Stevens turned down the stove's flame so his eggs cooked slowly and didn't burn. Fortunately, he had plenty of propane and wouldn't need his tanks serviced for a few more months.

The news coverage was enthralling but also overwhelming and he had work to do on his cabin, like fix a leak in the plumbing. The constant dripping was causing a tiny rivulet from beneath the cabin and watering the ferns outside. But that was life in the redwood forests of the Santa Cruz Mountains, just west of the Bay Area where all the craziness had gone down. Being out of the swamp was a relief. It was great to be back home in the trees and the fresh air. He stirred the eggs, rolled the sausage links one more time, and turned off the fire. Next was taking the orange juice from the refrigerator, drinking it down, and then pouring another cup of coffee.

Stevens gathered his food and picked up his fork when a loud knock at the door startled him. The *rap-rap-rap* made his heart skip a beat. Instinctively, he glanced at a cabinet where he kept one of his handguns. Then he peeked out the kitchen window, craning his neck to look right. It was a woman dressed in a flannel shirt, blue jeans, and hiking boots. She knocked again and he looked closer. She was the woman who lived in the adjacent lot through the grove of trees. He had never seen much of her, but he had only moved to the area several months earlier. He went to the front door and opened it.

"Hi there," he said.

"Oh, hi. I'm Amanda from next door."

"Yeah. I remember seeing you, passing through the woods. I'm Bob. Nice to meet you."

"We're neighbors. Well, kinda'. I mean… I live down near the end of this trail. You know, where that redwood fell last year, blocking the path. If you take the trail and go up the hill about a quarter of a mile – well that's me. Your closest neighbor."

"Good to know."

She sounded embarrassed. "Oh, my God. I'm so sorry to disturb you and I know I'm a ways away, but I was wondering if you might help me with something."

"Sure. If I can. What do you need?"

"I saw you hoofing in supplies last night and, well, I know this sounds silly but a bobcat got the last of my laying hens, and, well, I was wondering if I could borrow a couple of eggs. You're closer than driving to the store."

Bob laughed. "You don't have to borrow any. You can take a couple with you."

She was an attractive lady, mid-thirties with long blonde hair pulled back in a ponytail. Not the weekend warrior type. She looked comfortable in the setting and he immediately pictured her shooting, skinning, and dressing a deer with no hesitation. Yet, her smile and blue eyes were inviting.

"Come on in," he held the door open as she stepped inside.

He led the way to the kitchen where his eggs were lukewarm.

"Oh, I'm sorry. I interrupted your breakfast."

"No problem. Have a seat. Would you like some coffee?"

"That sounds great." She slid onto a chair and scooted forward to the kitchen table.

"So, what do you do, Amanda?" He grabbed a mug and poured her coffee.

"I'm a, well, let's just say I'm a software developer. Just working in Silicon Valley like so many others around here. Sometimes in person. Sometimes remotely, but out here I try to unplug as much as possible."

He was fine with the answer. He handed the mug to her and then sat at the table across from her. He didn't have to know anymore and if she wanted to tell him, she would. She looked more woodsy than she did nerdy, but what did a techie really look like anyway?

"How about you?" she asked.

"Investment broker. My own firm. Small. Actually, it's just me," he sighed. "Private clientele. I worked hard enough early on that I now just have a limited number of select portfolios and they keep me busy. Too busy, though." He sipped from his mug.

"Yeah, I notice you're gone a lot."

"You've been watching me?" He was concerned but played it off with a smile.

Amanda blushed. "No. I mean, yes, I mean—"

Stevens laughed. "No worries. I have to travel a lot. But I'd much rather be here doing nothing."

"Me, too." And then her eyes were sad. "I've been watching the news. I'm sure you've heard about the shooting."

"About Julius Brae? Yeah."

"How terrible. Just sickening."

Stevens thought through Brae's demeanor. He was brilliant, but arrogant. In an interview one time, the man bragged about how ProfileScene had so many users that the company was bigger and greater than the United States. But Stevens didn't feel sorry for the man. Hell, presidents had been assassinated before so why not corporate CEOs? Especially ones that were controlling people's right to free speech with their own ideologies.

"What have you heard?" asked Stevens.

"So far, they've ruled out nearly all employees. I guess there were protestors there?" She raised an eyebrow. "They're holding several of them for questioning. I hear the crime scene is massive and spread out everywhere."

"Yeah, that's pretty much what the news is saying."

"I can't believe someone could actually kill another human being like that." She waved a hand and shuddered. "I'm glad I wasn't in the office yesterday. Working from home sometimes has its perks, although the internet's a little spotty up here. I can deal with it because I hate the commute." She drank her coffee, took a calming breath, and changed the subject. "I can't believe that damn bobcat got some of my chickens. I guess no place is perfect, huh?"

"No, I guess not," he said. "How's the fencing around your coop?"

"Apparently not too good."

He chuckled. "Obviously."

"Hey." She spoke up in mock protest. "I can code software and run a trout line. But fencing? Just not my forte."

"How about if I check it out in a little bit?"

"That'd be great.

"But after breakfast." He got up, opened the refrigerator, and pulled out a carton. "You want eggs? I've got organic sausage, too. I'll fix some for you."

"I thought you'd never ask."

Stevens busied himself preparing breakfast.

Amanda was thinking. "ProfileScene is still offline. I guess the only positive about that is meeting a neighbor in person. Do you have a Profile page?"

"Nope, sure don't," said Stevens breaking eggs, stirring them into the pan, and adding sausage.

"Oh?"

"You're surprised?" Stevens smiled. "No, I'm not a social media fan. I deal with my clients online when I have to. Mostly emails. But when it comes to personal friendships, I like them in real life. Old school, right?"

Amanda smiled. "Yeah, nothing beats real-life friendships."

CHAPTER FOUR

Stone looked at Jake who was walking out from beneath the freeway underpass and stopped when he reached the spot where the victim had fallen, a large grassy patch. A rare sliver of green running along the sidewalk. Kilbraide was to the north, about twenty yards away along Riverside Drive.

The crime scene had been cleared earlier and the trio had returned to double-check the report and go over their findings.

Jake glanced to Stone and then Kilbraide. "It's feasible."

"That the shot could come from that angle?" asked Stone. "What do you think, Kilbraide?"

Kilbraide walked back to Stone. "Yeah, I think it's possible."

The area was trashy from years of neglect. The victim had no ID and no belongings other than the clothes he'd been wearing. He wasn't connected with any missing person reports and he didn't look like he was homeless.

"It could have been a drive-by shooting, even a random shooting," said Kilbraide. "You know, some kids in a car looking for a thrill or gangbangers initiating a new member. They're driving by, drinking, maybe a little high, they've been laughing and bragging about who's the toughest and they see this guy strolling near the overpass. Maybe he was out for a breath of fresh air or walking his dog. Any reports of missing dogs?"

"None that we've been told," said Jake. "My thought is that any car would have to come from the east." He pointed along the street. "With the way the body fell, it was a clear shot and a quick getaway and no cross traffic to worry about."

Stone studied the surroundings. The freeway was elevated up an embankment and crossed over Lankershim Boulevard. A gas station was at the corner of Lankershim and Riverside Drive and a thrift store was directly across the street, along with a handful of other retail shops. Apartments stood further down. "Any luck with the surveillance from those places?"

"So far nothing," said Kilbraide.

Stone was frustrated. "The victim had no tattoos or gang markings of any kind. Just a twenty-something man who either got what someone thought he deserved or just happened to be in the wrong place at the wrong time."

A sound of engines drawing close interrupted the investigation. Two black SUVs pulled along the curb and rolled to a stop. Black SUVs always meant trouble. Stone tensed and readied to grab his handgun as the doors opened. Men in suits and ties got out. "Hello, gentlemen. We're here to talk to Detective Brian Kilbraide."

"And you are—?" Stone kept his hand near his firearm.

"Special Agent Tommy Markus, FBI." He flipped open his badge with the title Supervisory Special Agent.

Jake wasn't impressed. "Special Agent? Aren't you all special agents? That diminishes the word special. Are there regular agents and maybe Not-So-Special-Agents?"

"You must be Detective Jake Sharpe."

"You're right. How about Special Detective Sharpe? Has a nice ring to it."

Stone jumped in. "I'm Detective Tom Stone, LAPD. And we're in the middle of an investigation here."

"Cool. Making progress?" Markus looked around the grassy area.

"Of a sort, yeah."

The other agents stepped forward and flanked Marcus who eyed Kilbraide. "Through the power of deductive reasoning, you must be Kilbraide."

"It's Detective Kilbraide."

"Alright, Detective Kilbraide."

"What's going on?" asked Stone.

Markus mimicked Stone. "We're in the middle of an investigation as well."

"If it has anything to do with my detectives, then you better be more forthcoming." Stone was annoyed and locked eyes with Markus.

"I don't want to interfere with your work, Detective Stone, but we've got our own dilemma we're trying to solve."

"What does that have to do with him?" Jake waved his thumb toward Kilbraide.

Agent Markus was poker-faced and non-committal. "Like I said, it's official business. We just have some questions."

"Well, then ask your questions and get the hell out of here," said Stone. "You're disturbing our crime scene."

"Detective Stone, this isn't the time or place for a pissing match. You have no authority to tell me what I can and cannot do."

Jake joked with Stone. "He certainly sounds official."

"And whether you like it or not," Markus continued, "we're taking Kilbraide—

Kilbraide interrupted. "That's Detective Kilbraide."

"—in for questioning."

They locked eyes again.

"You're taking one of my men," said Stone, "so I should at least be informed of what's going on."

"I'd love to sit down and tell you all about it, even have a beer on the government's tab. But everything's unfolding pretty fast. And, Detective Stone, you know as well as I do that we can't discuss an ongoing investigation."

"What's unfolding?" asked Jake.

"That's what we need to ask Detective Kilbraide."

"I understand that," said Stone. "But you know, we're on the same side, so you can't just show up and take one of my guys without a damn good reason. How about a little professional courtesy, agency to agency, and tell me what the reason is?"

Agent Markus relaxed. "You said that quite well, Detective. You're right. We do have a damned good reason."

"Yeah, I'd like to know what that is, too," said Kilbraide.

"I'm not at liberty to say," Marcus softened his tone, "but it may have something to do with that matter of killing Julius Brae. Maybe it does. Maybe it doesn't."

"What?" Kilbraide was shocked.

"What the hell are you talking about?" asked Jake.

Stone stood speechless.

"Okay. From one agency to another, and we're all professionals here, and you didn't hear this from me, but your name, Detective Kilbraide, was written on the back of a patch that was found in what we believe was the shooter's hide in a swampy area, just less than a mile from ProfileScene's main campus."

"A patch?" Kilbraide looked shaken.

"Yeah." Agent Markus motioned to the SUVs. "We got a few questions to ask you. Time is of the essence."

"What kind of patch? What'd it say?" asked Stone.

"*One Shot, One Kill. No Remorse. I Decide.*"

Jake looked as stunned as Stone and looked to Kilbraide. "My God. Do you think your boy is back?"

"He's not my boy," grumbled Kilbraide.

Markus addressed Stone. "Detective Stone, I've put in a request for files on that unsolved sniper case you guys had." Markus motioned for Kilbraide to follow him. "We've got a lot of information to go over, Detective. But right now, we want to know why your name is on the back of the patch."

Kilbraide looked at Stone. "What do I do?"

"I guess you got to go."

"This sucks," muttered Kilbraide, following Marcus to the SUVs.

Stone and Jake watched as the agents drove away.

"Well, hell, that was unexpected." Jake was stunned.

"Yeah, sure was," Stone agreed. "Something doesn't smell right."

CHAPTER FIVE

A massive headache gripped Kilbraide during a session of grueling questioning that lasted for hours. He knew nothing about his name on the patch and had never received any word, hint, and had no knowledge that the shooting was about to take place, especially an attack that mirrored similar murders in Los Angeles that Kilbraide had investigated.

"You got anything else?" asked Agent Marcus, drilling him.

"Nothing further. You now know everything I know."

He had never expected to be at the mercy of the FBI and wondered if Uncle Sam's boys were going to comb through his phone records, emails, and computer hard drive. He could care less if they did, but a slight cloud of suspicion hung over him because his name was linked to an atrocity. And his fear was that some idiot could plant a piece of evidence, use him as a scapegoat, and make his life a living hell.

And then Marcus informed him that he was going to take a leave of absence from the LAPD and assist in the Julius Brae shooting as a

Special Advisor. The icing on the proverbial cake was that they were flying to the Bay Area.

"I checked your records and see that you had quite a few kills as a sniper in the service."

"It was the best way I could serve my country." He didn't want to say any more than what was necessary.

"So that means you know something about tracking your target and taking them out?"

"The military put me where they needed me and I exceeded their expectations. I saved a lot of lives in my unit."

"The FBI needs you now," said Marcus. "I want you on the front line with us. The Bureau's sharpshooters are the best. I'd put them up against anybody, but this shooter made a connection with you, and, honestly, I want to know why. I expect you'll help us out."

"I guess there won't be any sightseeing at Fisherman's Wharf."

"Unless the sight you see there is whoever pulled the trigger on Julius Brae. This is purely a working trip."

"How soon do we leave?" asked Kilbraide.

"Now."

***

Kilbraide couldn't shake the feeling that society was sinking fast. Murky water pooled near his feet while he studied the distance from under the bridge and across the open area to ProfileScene's sprawling main campus. Despite technology's tools making life easier and more convenient, it seemed that the world was sicker than ever.

Special Agent Marcus stood by his side as he studied the swamp while forensics teams continued to search for clues.

"The patch was discovered here?" asked Kilbraide. A pop-up tent lay on its side, partly caught in the bushes.

"That's right," said Marcus.

"And you believe this is where the shooter was?"

"Yep. Process of elimination. All neighboring buildings were combed through. Nothing. Ballistics traced the trajectory to this spot. And you're standing in what's left of the shooter's encampment. The homeless pretty much scavenged everything before we got here."

"Including obliterating any evidence."

"We found that tent, or what's left of it, and inside was the patch with your name on it."

"And that's the reason I'm here," sighed Kilbraide.

"Don't worry, we'll find more clues. My guys are good."

"If you say so."

Marcus looked from the bridge to the distant complex. "That's one hell of a shot from here. It's one thing if they're using a rocket launcher, but this was dead on, ignore the pun."

"Ignored. And, yeah, it's a hell of a shot for nearly everyone who's alive on planet Earth." Kilbraide thought of the sniper that he had tracked in Los Angeles, whose targets were killed in seemingly safe spaces like home, church, and a public horse-riding trail.

"Could you do it?" asked Marcus, interrupting Kilbraide's train of thought.

"What kind of question is that?" He was taken aback and didn't like what his answer might imply.

"Could you make a shot from this angle and this distance?"

"It would take incredible planning and patience."

"But you could do it, right?"

Kilbraide felt uneasy, like he was being questioned as a suspect. He shrugged off the question and didn't answer.

"Would this guy have had a spotter?"

Kilbraide pondered the question. "Unlikely."

"Good, I see we're on the same page. The homeless we've been questioning said there was only one man living here."

"I'm not surprised that the shooter chose it. It's a great location. A perfect hide. He lives here a while. Blends in. Studies his target. And when the timing's just right, he sends the round. Then as all hell breaks loose, he disappears back into the scenery. It's what he, or we rather, were trained to do."

"We know it was a high caliber round, but what are your thoughts? We don't have a lot to go on here. So, if this is the same guy from your case in LA, tell me, what's he got? What's in his kit? Any info's going to help us."

"Just basic. A scope. A quality weapon. A wind gauge." Kilbraide thought about how ingenious the setup was. "And one other thing."

"What's that?"

"One hell of a motive. We have to ask the most important question: why Brae?"

"You're not telling me anything I don't already know," said Marcus. "Look, I've interviewed some of our top FBI marksmen and got technical info out of them. But even that's more than you're giving me. I recruited you for a reason. Your knowledge. Your expertise. Your insight. We think this is your guy. So help us out here."

Kilbraide paced the area. Stench lingered over the top of the stagnant water. "This wasn't just a well-planned, by the numbers, technical assassination. The shooter had to become part of the event."

"Are you kidding me with all that *namaste* one-with-the-world shit?"

A shout rang out from the edges of the muddy water. "You looking for Grunt?"

Kilbraide turned to see a skinny man with a shaggy beard duck under the yellow crime scene tape and stumble up the path. The man looked as steady as a feather blowing in a tornado. Kilbraide put a hand on his weapon that was hidden beneath his jacket. "Looking for who?"

"Grunt. The guy who lived here. I talked to him. Nice guy. Is he in trouble?" The skinny guy's eyes darted from one person to another.

Marcus studied the man. "And who are you?"

"They call me Skinny Guy, 'cause I'm skinny. Some call me Bonesy. I live around here sometimes. Your guys down there," he pointed along the path, "told me to come talk to you."

"I'm Detective Kilbraide and this is Special Agent Marcus."

Skinny Guy grinned as he looked from Kilbraide to Marcus. "Special? What makes you so special?"

Marcus ignored the jab. "You know who was living here?"

"Yeah, Grunt."

"Grunt? That's what he went by?"

"That's what he said his name was. But I think they just called him that because he grunts a lot. Or he was in the military. Yeah, grunts. That's what they call them jarheads in the Marines."

"Did he tell you that he was a Marine?" asked Kilbraide.

"No, he just grunted a lot. But I can always tell. He just had that look." Skinny Guy focused on Kilbraide and narrowed his eyes. "Kinda' like you. You guys are a lot alike."

"How so?"

"You both look the same. You got an attitude." Skinny Guy held up his hands in a reassuring way. "You know that tough guy, military way of acting. And an aura shimmering around you like—"

"Like what?" asked Marcus.

"Calm. Self-confident. Like ain't nothing bothering you. Ya know, I served, too."

"Always nice to meet a brother in arms. What branch did you serve in?" asked Kilbraide.

"Army. Salvation Army." Skinny Guy laughed. "I served breakfast there this morning."

"Alright Mr. Funny Pants, what else can you tell us?" Marcus was pissed off.

"I don't know. You got a smoke?"

"No, but I'll buy you a pack," said Kilbraide.

Marcus opened his mouth to object, but Kilbraide gave him a look.

"Thanks. See, you're nice just like Grunt. He gave me a whole bag of cans and shit to recycle. I think I was buggin' him though and he was just tryin' to get rid of me. Can't blame 'em."

"What else?" asked Kilbraide.

"You guys both look like you pump iron. Same skin tone, same—"

"Grunt was Black?" asked Marcus.

"Yeah. What of it?"

"Okay, we'll get a full description from you, but, when was the last time you saw him?"

"The day that super-computer nerd got killed." Skinny Guy held up his fingers like a gun. "Blam."

Kilbraide thought the skinny guy was a wealth of knowledge. "Can you tell me if he, if Grunt, was acting suspicious, was—"

"He's homeless. Like me. We're always acting suspicious."

"Was Grunt doing anything out of the ordinary?" Kilbraide pressed. "Did you see anything?"

"Yeah, he had some funny-looking thing on his shopping cart. He said it was a weathervane."

"A weathervane?" asked Marcus.

Skinny Guy furrowed his brow. "Yeah, I didn't stutter. Oh, and he got a text on his phone while we were talking. And—wait a minute." Skinny Guy took a breath. "You don't think that he—no, dude, he didn't have no gun or anything. He's a nice guy. Gave me his cans. But when I left, he didn't see me, but I looked back and saw him digging in the ground. Right over there near them reeds."

Kilbraide and Marcus looked to where he pointed.

"But I didn't think nothing of it. We ain't got no safe place out here to keep our stuff, which I call valuables. You'd be surprised how much shit is buried out here."

"I don't think I want to know. So he got a text?" asked Kilbraide.

"Yeah, and don't ask me from who. How the hell would I know?"

"And you haven't seen him since then?"

"No. Anyway, I had come back. After recycling I got some CBD, the best stuff. King Moses CBD. I was going to give Grunt a little. Said his shoulder was hurting."

"Which one?" asked Kilbraide, thinking back to when he shot Stevens in the murky waters of Balboa Park in Los Angeles.

"The one connected to his arm." Skinny guy huffed. "I don't know which one. Can I continue?"

"Go ahead."

"I was getting worried about him; he left his tent and shit. Well, there was more stuff, but you know, around here, things disappear quickly. And the next thing I know, you guys show up with your yellow tape." Skinny Guy eyed Marcus and Kilbraide. "Now I think you think Grunt did somethin'. Dude, I ain't talkin' no more. He was a nice guy. Gave me his cans."

"Can you remember anything else about the last time you saw him?" asked Marcus.

"No. How many times you going to ask me the same damn question? But it was God-awful noisy after I headed to recycling. I heard sirens and saw helicopters flying all around them buildings over there. But that's not my business, I stay away from cops."

Marcus pointed out the obvious. "Do you?"

"Hey, I was just coming over here to see if you knew anything about Grunt and make sure he was okay." He shifted from one foot to another and turned to Kilbraide. "Man, I don't want to talk no more. How about them smokes?"

"Sure. Come on."

Kilbraide led Skinny Guy down the path, asked a few more questions, and gave him his business card. "If you think of anything, or if you see anything, give me a call." Kilbraide reached in his pocket and pulled out a twenty. "Smoking's not good for you. Get yourself something to eat."

"Dude, I appreciate it. Oh, yeah." Skinny Guy looked like he was thinking. "Sure, I'll get myself something to eat. Yeah, right." He pocketed the bill and headed down the path.

Kilbraide watched and then headed back to the scene.

"You can't give them money," said Marcus.

"Who can't?"

"The FBI doesn't do that."

Kilbraide smiled. "Yeah, right. Well, I do things different. Besides, I'm not FBI. Just here as a *Special Advisor*. Remember?"

"All right. I didn't see it."

They walked over to the reeds, looked closely, and Kilbraide saw where the ground was uneven, like it had been disturbed.

"Did he say anything else?" asked Marcus.

"No, just said our shooter really looked healthy."

Kilbraide knelt and studied the distance from the tent to the ProfileScene building. Besides himself, he only knew one other person that could make that shot. The man he'd hunted down before, Bob Stevens.

CHAPTER SIX

Drizzle fell through the redwoods as Bob Stevens pulled out of his driveway in his pick-up truck. He had the wipers on intermittently to wipe away the light rain as he drove through town. A little further along the winding road there were the red and blue flashing lights of a police cruiser. Stevens took a breath but immediately calmed himself as he pulled up to a policewoman who was dressed in a rain slicker. She held up her hand and motioned for Stevens to stop.

He tapped the brakes on the wet, mountain road. She took a few steps toward his car and motioned to a line of cars in the opposite lane. It was an accident scene. The policewoman waved the cars through in the uphill lane and after a dozen went by, she motioned for Stevens to move on. He caught a glimpse of the problem as he drove slowly by.

A car had slammed into an embankment. A tow truck driver was fastening a line to the car while the driver stood nearby and tapped the keys of her cell phone. Communication was so much easier now than it had ever been in human history, thought Stevens, thanks to algorithms, coding, and lightning-fast search functions that put information at the fingertips of so many. Too bad most just used it for texting and sending memes while driving.

He steered carefully around the tow truck and wondered about all the technology that was going to waste. All you had to do was press a button to have a voice and think that you're somebody, an influencer, somebody who makes a difference.

But then there were too many people who lost their minds over trivial issues. They spewed their hatred toward anyone who didn't agree with them, and Stevens saw that hatred ruining the country he loved. The most recent action that shook him was journalists who had no moral code and sensationalized a story on U.S. troop movements in the Middle East. The leaks led to an ambush that claimed a dozen American lives. Leaks and lies were now acceptable to publish, and the public never questioned them. Sickening.

Stevens drove on and took an exit toward the northern part of Silicon Valley.

The worst offender was the flamboyant Senator from the region, Faisel Alanasian, who callously said the public had a right to know what the troops were doing on the taxpayer's dime. He was famous for accusing the military and anyone else who didn't agree with him of racism, white supremacy, and using hate speech.

He was home from D.C. for a round of fundraising dinners, blathering about taxing others to share their wealth while he pushed policies to buy the votes of executives during lunchtime photo ops in his district office.

Alanasian's family immigrated from Armenia to California where he was born. After college, he interned on Capitol Hill, stayed close to the Bay Area's political scene, and secured government funding to build numerous businesses that were never profitable. But the façade paid off. Now, reaching sixty years old, his own social media was filled with hugs from celebrities and corporate scions who voted him into office while he proclaimed the glory of a benevolent government over the worth of an individual. A closet socialist wanting nothing more than to line his own pockets while pretending to care about the needy. Disgusting. Of course, the Hollywood elite were among the rich and powerful who hung on his every word and were begging him to run for president.

Today, lunchtime would eliminate that possibility.

Steven's phone was mounted on the dashboard and vibrated with a cryptic text message. *Green light.* The plan was in motion. Everything was ready. Stevens had his gear stored carefully behind his seat in a hidden compartment.

He blanked his mind and tuned out the world, driving at a slow and steady rhythm. There was no need to rush. Other cars sped by. Let them go. This was a moment for him to sink into his own self and find that peace that was so beautiful. Until another thought jolted him. Amanda's eyes during breakfast a few days earlier. He brought his years of discipline acquired through hardships in the military to bear and pushed thoughts of her aside. Her smile. And her hair. Everything about her crept back in. Thoughts turned to his late wife, a woman who had a winning smile and natural elegance. Until she—*Face the reality*, he thought. Until she got hooked on drugs starting at a party with friends, then spiraled out of control for the next few years and died from an overdose.

No. *Don't get sucked in.*

Amanda was a foreign substance contaminating his mentality. He didn't need the distraction. "Out. Get out of my head."

Frustrated, he forced himself back to visualizing the process and procedures again and again. He pulled off the highway and drove toward an older section of town that had seen better days. Re-development left this area neglected while other neighborhoods were on the *chic* list. He pulled into a rundown parking garage that was one of the first places to have security cameras throughout. Stevens drove to the second level and pulled alongside an old compact car. Intel confirmed the cameras in this area didn't work. He parked his truck, transferred his equipment that was conveniently clustered in a backpack, and sat in the cramped driver's seat of the small car. He looked around the cavernous space of the structure and after seeing no one, he started the engine and took off.

The collaboration with the Agency was perfected on various assignments through the years. He didn't ask questions but followed orders like a true patriot. They had a mission and believed, just like Stevens believed.

He pulled up to a curb near a gas station, parked, and put a couple of quarters in the meter. He checked his watch, grabbed his backpack, then walked one block to a light rail station. He knew that video cameras were used for safety and knew their range, so he walked as much as he could in a crowd and shielded his face from view as he boarded the train. He got off two stops later in a renovated commercial district with a mixture of live-work lofts, trendy cafes, and condos crammed into every building on one side of the tracks. On the other side, the city planners kept the green of nature where hiking trails wound up the hills into wooded areas.

Only minutes to go, but that was enough time for Stevens to feel like he was in a meditative state as he hiked up a little-used trail. He walked off the path and found his hide, a grove of California scrub oaks with thick trunks and gnarly branches nestled between two large boulders. The stand of trees would help deaden any sound. Alanasian's building across the tracks stood like a beacon in the midst of the commercial district. Adjacent was a handball court. It was built with a federal grant that was supposed to be used for disadvantaged kids. And it was—once every few months for photo ops.

Everything had been planned through previous scouting trips. The target was exactly 1,436 yards away.

He scanned the area below. Nothing but some joggers and most of them had their ears plugged with earbuds. People wandered in and out of the train station, while shoppers headed into overpriced boutiques. Life was normal.

He unzipped his backpack and set the wind meter on a flat rock. Then in a series of clicks, he assembled the rifle, attached the sound suppressor to the end of the muzzle, adjusted the optics on the pic rail, and attached the bipod.

Cars and trucks on the streets looked small and vulnerable, just like Alanasian did as he stepped outside of his office onto the handball court wearing his trademark workout shorts and a polo shirt. He always played a round of handball right before heading back into the office for a meal and the rest of the day's tasks. Men and women were stationed around the perimeter of the court, trying to look casual as they guarded his life. But they were totally unaware of what was waiting in the hills.

Stevens clutched the rifle, sunk into a blissful state of nothingness, and looked through the riflescope. Alanasian chatted with someone near him as he tossed the rubber handball up and down in an extra moment of his life that was given like a gift.

He took the Hornaday 338 bullet from his pouch, pulled back the bolt, inserted the round, and then worked the bolt forward, ready for action. Stevens accounted for the wind, took a breath, opened his mouth slightly, and as he was about to squeeze the trigger, Alanasian's girlfriend who was half his age sashayed onto the court, exclaimed something, and danced around waving her hands. Her newest diamond necklace must not be fitting well, mused Stevens who checked his watch and hoped he had put enough in the parking meter.

Alanasian handed the woman a wad of cash, kissed her, patted her ass, and sent her on her way so he could get back to his game. This was it.

Stevens steadied his breath, acquired his target, and as Alanasian joked with a nearby guard, he squeezed the trigger. In one-point-five seconds the bullet struck, tearing the wealthy man apart. The people around the senator immediately hit the ground, ran inside, or dashed in circles waving their arms and screaming. So much for the guards around the perimeter. The only emotion Stevens felt was that of a job well done. He congratulated himself silently and retraced his actions. The gun was immediately dismantled and placed into the bag with the rangefinder, riflescope, and anemometer. There was one thing left to do.

He pulled a patch from his pocket, scribbled on it, and tacked it onto the trunk of a tree.

How was it so damned simple?

Stevens walked away from under cover of the oaks, reconnected with a part of the trail that was hidden from view below, and returned to the train station. Sirens suddenly split the air and police cruisers flashing red and blue lights zipped down the street. The chaos reached a fevered pitch while Stevens waited calmly for the train that pulled up within minutes. He boarded the light rail, was whisked away to his original stop, and headed to his compact car. He arrived just as the parking meter expired. Stevens glanced at his watch.

One minute off, I'm getting rusty.

The streets were nearly empty and the drive back to the old garage was easy. He drove to the second level, parked beside his truck, and stashed his backpack in the hidden compartment. Stevens grabbed his phone and texted one familiar word: *Done.*

He pulled away and the robotic side of his personality that enabled him to take down a target suddenly had a fleeting moment of uncertainty, almost like a feeling of guilt. It was so damn confusing until a thought of Amanda standing on his porch and knocking on his door floated into his mind.

He fought back a smile.

CHAPTER SEVEN

This was the Silicon Valley tour from hell, Kilbraide thought, sitting in the passenger seat and cradling the phone against one ear while Special Agent Marcus drove as quickly as he could.

Stone was on the line. "Stevens was pissed off about drug financiers. I can't find anything that remotely ties Julius Brae to drugs. Who knows what you'd have to dig through to find anything on Alanasian."

Marcus was annoyed and spoke sharply to Kilbraide who tried to play it cool and glance out the window. "You're working with me at my direction. Hang up. The LAPD has enough problems of their own."

Kilbraide finished up his conversation with Stone. "Yeah, Stone, that's what I was wondering. I've got to get going here. If you come up with anything, then let me know."

"In that case," said Stone, "you probably won't be hearing from me or Jake any time soon."

Kilbraide hung up and spoke to Marcus. "Just using my resources."

"Ask me first." Marcus turned a corner and into a parking lot where they passed an army of news trucks. Cameramen and journalists were prepping for live reports and waiting for the next official briefing while they speculated on the motive and made-up narratives of an unknown suspect.

Marcus parked, reached in the back seat, grabbed a windbreaker emblazoned with the FBI logo across the back, and handed it to Kilbraide. "Now that you're one of us, put this on."

"One of who?"

"Us."

Kilbraide got out and put on the jacket. "You make me feel special."

"Let's go," said Marcus, zipping the bottom half of his windbreaker.

They headed past the crime scene barrier to police officers gathered around the handball court.

The senator's body lay covered.

Death was like an ignition key for an engine. Turn it on and a host of specialists raced into action. The FBI's photographers clicked away recording the exact position of the body while the coroner's office checked for time of death. The obvious cause was a gun blast that also raised numerous questions and clues: where did the bullet enter? How was he standing? Who shot him and why?

Weeping and sobbing staff were answering questions while wiping their eyes and blowing their noses. There was only one shot, from what they could tell. Someone else thought there may have been a second. But it could have been an echo off the walls of the handball court. A witness said they saw people ducking and running away across the street. Someone else said they saw a scary looking White person running toward the area with what looked like a handgun. That turned out to be the first police officer on the scene. He'd been on break at the coffee shop next door when he heard the shot.

Rational people who had been calm and standing around the senator or sitting behind their desks and doing their work moments earlier, now had different recollections of the shooting. Some held onto their preconceived notions of what happened while others chatted as excitedly as the whirring blades of a high-speed blender. Some were physically shaking. No one in this high-tech corridor of power knew anything about assassinations. They were caught off guard and catapulted into a foreign world beyond their control.

A kill shot. Kilbraide studied the different angles. Office buildings several stories high were nearby, but a shot from one of the windows was unlikely—no clear egress for the shooter. The street was now blocked off and sealed tight, but firing from a moving vehicle would have been impossible given where the court was located. Kilbraide glanced across the street, beyond the light rail station, and up into the hills.

Marcus was standing nearby when a radio attached to his coat sounded and a tinny voice came through.

"We've got something. Come take a look."

The voice came from across the street and up the side of the hill where Kilbraide had been looking. Hiking trails lined the slope and a nearby park. Now he wanted nothing more than to have Stone and Jake standing there with him, drawing from their wealth of experience, confidence, and determination. But instead, he was stuck in 'Frisco with a bunch of Feds.

"Let's go." Marcus motioned for Kilbraide to follow across the street, past the train station, and up one of the hiking trails.

Police, FBI agents and Crime Scene Investigators were fanned out everywhere, looking closely through the weeds and among the boulders. Marcus and Kilbraide moved quickly toward a grove of trees where an Agent was photographing the trunk of a California oak. Marcus looked first, studied it, and then stepped aside for Kilbraide to see.

It was a patch. And Kilbraide's name was scrawled on it.

"What the hell?" Kilbraide was shaken.

"The shooter is as fixated on you as he is on his victims." Marcus glanced down the slope toward the office complex.

Kilbraide didn't respond. He fought to keep cool and think through the important details. But he kept thinking, *What the hell is Stevens up to?*

"I see your brain working. Is there something you should be telling me?" asked Marcus.

Before Kilbraide could respond, a voice called out. "Agent Marcus." A woman in slacks and a long-sleeve dress shirt made her way into the gathering. She acted like the leader of the pack with a half dozen, heavily armed agents flanking her. She reached in her pocket and flashed an ID badge. *National Intelligence Authority.*

Marcus narrowed his eyes. "And you are?"

"Agent Jenna Catalonia. I need Detective Brian Kilbraide." Her voice was no nonsense.

"You do, huh?" Marcus studied the agents closely. His protest was weak. "Under whose authority?"

"Someone way above your pay grade." She looked to Kilbraide. "With me." She turned to leave, expecting her demand to be obeyed.

"Wait. What?" Kilbraide was confused.

"I got a lot more questions," Marcus protested. "You can't just take my advisor."

Catalonia stopped, looked back, and responded coldly. "I can and I will. If you don't like it, then take it up with your superiors." She had a bronze complexion, hair pulled back in a ponytail, and a clearly defined jawline. Kilbraide envisioned her hands used as a lethal weapon. She was clearly a woman you didn't mess with.

Marcus was puzzled. "Wait, I, uh, I'm going to file a complaint."

"Why bother?" said Catalonia, handing her card to Marcus. "You need to bag and tag all the evidence and I expect a report by the end of the day." She turned to Kilbraide. "Time's in short supply. Let's go."

She motioned down the hill to a cluster of black SUVs parked near the rail station. Armed guards stood watch around the vehicles.

Kilbraide hesitated and looked from Agent Catalonia to Agent Marcus. "What do I do?"

"Guess there's no choice. You got to go." Marcus rolled his eyes and kicked the dirt.

"Do I keep the jacket?" Kilbraide smiled.

"No." Marcus was serious.

Kilbraide took it off and tossed it. "Here you go."

Marcus caught it and Kilbraide turned to Catalonia. "You got a windbreaker I can wear?"

She was annoyed. "We don't do jackets."

Kilbraide headed back down the hill with Catalonia and her guards. One thought was beating in his mind: *this is the wildest ride of my life.*

CHAPTER EIGHT

Kilbraide stayed calm as the convoy of SUVs sped along. A man who had stood guard now sat with him in the back while in the front passenger seat Catalonia checked her phone. Her eyes were glued to the screen.

The man looked bored as he stared out the window. Kilbraide initially suspected that the mob had captured him. Conspiracy theories aside, he assured himself that only government agents acted like this. Catalonia's tapping on her cell phone and the *whirr* of the tires on the freeway were the only sounds. She wasn't offering any explanation of where they were driving or saying who she actually was. Kilbraide enjoyed studying her face, trying to pick up on any facial clues. Her eyes and other features were quite pleasant, and only reinforced that she was in charge. She had just kidnapped him moments ago, and already he was attracted to her. *Stockholm Syndrome.* He amused himself with the thought as one mile blurred into another.

He noted the scenery and tried to spot landmarks to get an idea of where they were headed, but it all flew by. Then he saw a cyclone fence and an Air National Guard plane in the distance. An airport. The SUVs turned left and drove past signs warning drivers not to trespass. Kilbraide thought they were heading onto the same federal airport he had flown into with the FBI, but it wasn't. He guessed they were in the southern portion of the Bay Area.

They drove up to armed guards who recognized the vehicle, raised the barriers, and waved them through. The driver continued onto the tarmac and stopped in front of an oversized hangar that was used to house dirigibles during World War Two. The door was opened and a tug tractor was towing a sleek, all black, three-engine private jet outside. There were no tail markings or any other identifying symbols on the jet. *Who are these people?*

A man and woman wearing khakis and dark shirts stood with a clipboard, checking off items as they viewed the plane. They must be the pilots, thought Kilbraide.

"Get ready to fly." Catalonia looked back at Kilbraide as she opened her door.

"Are checked bags extra?" asked Kilbraide.

"You don't have any so you're in luck." Catalonia got out and busily tapped the keys on her phone.

Kilbraide opened his door and as soon as his feet hit the ground, the man who was sitting next to him in the SUV was now standing a little too close for comfort. *At least they think I'm important.*

Catalonia gave the pilots a command as she passed by. "Wheels up in five."

"Yes, ma'am. You got it."

The tug released the jet and the pilots boarded.

"You don't really use that cliché movie-speak, do you?" Kilbraide asked her.

A smile almost cracked her hard exterior. "I suggest you get on board, Detective Kilbraide."

Kilbraide thought how nice Catalonia would look if she smiled, but she was busy on her phone, dialing, and then talking to someone. A U.S. senator was just shot dead so she could be forgiven for being all work, but he knew nothing about her, the strange, unmarked plane, or the entourage of military-like personnel surrounding them. At least they were standing on the property of the federal government—or at least he thought so.

Catalonia finished with her call, pocketed the phone, and spoke to Kilbraide with authority. "Let's go."

The engines spun to life.

The woman was a perpetual ball of energy as she headed up the few steps. Kilbraide followed, liking how she moved. The low ceiling forced him to bend slightly as he entered the craft. There were two sofas in the middle of the plane in addition to six seats facing forward and workstations filled with what looked to be surveillance and communication equipment.

"Sit over there." Catalonia pointed to the first row, which only had two seats.

"Aye, aye, Captain." Kilbraide settled next to the window and watched as the grounds crew gave the craft a final check. The man who had been guarding Kilbraide in the SUV waited for the rest of the personnel to board the craft and take their places. Then he climbed in and closed the door, sealing them in tight.

Within seconds, the plane was rolling forward.

"Do you mind if I ask where we're going?" Kilbraide looked at Catalonia who took a seat next to him.

"No, I don't mind." Her jaw was set, but she didn't offer any information.

Kilbraide was annoyed and looked out the window. The plane lined up, paused, then immediately screamed down the runway, pushing him back in his seat. It lifted off and the Bay Area came into view. The jet banked one way, then another, and a slight nausea hit him. He wished he had his sea-bands to fight the dizziness. The aircraft then headed straight over land and into the clouds. Kilbraide took a breath, felt better, and was ready to give Catalonia a piece of his mind for keeping him in the dark, but when he looked her way she smiled.

"You okay?" she asked.

"Just peachy."

"I got to hand it to you," she said. "You really go with the flow."

Kilbraide was taken aback. "Do I have a choice?"

"No." She was totally composed and seemed quite pleasant for a moment.

For some strange reason, he thought of the murder investigation that Stone and Jake were handling in LA. That was a run of the mill killing that probably didn't even get attention in San Fernando Valley's *Daily News.*

"Look, I know this is happening at a dizzying speed for you."

Kilbraide glanced around. "More like lightning speed. Like this jet. What is it?"

"Classified."

"Okay. We're off to a good start."

Catalonia kept her seat belt low and tight. "All right. Some background. We had picked up a lot of chatter, but, unfortunately, we couldn't decipher it before Julius Brae, and now, Senator Alanasian were killed."

"We?"

"Classified."

"Okay. Then tell me what you can tell me."

"It's all classified."

"Then why—"

Catalonia was impatient. "Are you going to keep interrupting me or may I continue?"

"Please continue."

"Thank you. You'll have to sign a binding NDA and you'll be given clearance on a need-to-know basis."

Kilbraide waited a beat. "What do I need to know?"

The craft bumped slightly as it reached its cruising altitude.

"Let's start with Brae. Just like Alanasian, it was a strategic killing. A big difference was there was a crowd at the first one. We interrogated the protestors, none of them were armed, and except for a few minor black marks, their dossiers were clean."

"Dossiers?"

"On everybody. But classified. And there was absolutely no destruction on ProfileScene's campus. Not even spray-painted graffiti. The protestors also gave conflicting testimonies on who was organizing the event. But they all confirmed that they were paid to meet at a predetermined location in San Francisco that morning, and then they would be bussed to the protest."

Kilbraide thought about it. "They were a front?"

"Some had legitimate gripes, like the standard, big-corporations-taking-away-our-freedoms kind of thing. But overall, they were a distraction for the assassination."

"So what am I doing here?"

"Your name was on the patch, both of them. And this has all the earmarks of the sniper you tracked in LA."

"Bob Stevens."

"Bingo. He's the one."

The jet dipped in an air pocket before gaining altitude and rising above the scattered clouds. Kilbraide glanced below. The urban sprawl had given way to desert and dry-looking mountains.

"This thing's moving along at a pretty good clip, isn't it?" he remarked.

"You better believe it. I'm sure you noticed this isn't your normal private jet."

Obviously. Kilbraide noticed the guards quietly talking among themselves and the technicians monitoring the surveillance consoles. "Does that mean I don't have to pay for my drinks?"

"You want a bottle of water?" asked Catalonia.

"Do I get bread with it?"

"You're not a prisoner."

"I prefer a soda."

Catalonia motioned to the guard who got up and headed to the galley.

Kilbraide re-imagined tracking Stevens through the swamp near LA's Sepulveda Dam, shooting him, and looking in his face as the medics came and tended to him. There was a look of respect in the man's eyes.

The guard returned with drinks. "You like Ginger Ale? That's all we got."

"Yeah, I can handle it." Kilbraide took the can. "The ginger will be good for my stomach."

The man handed a bottle of water to Catalonia.

"So how much do you know about Stevens?" asked Kilbraide.

"We wanted to ask you the same thing."

Kilbraide opened the can, took a sip, and stretched his legs. He looked at the bottle. "Tastes better in a bottle." He went back to the topic. "Do you know the day after I shot him, we went to question him at the hospital and guess what we found?"

Catalonia sipped her water and remained completely calm like she was holding court. "An empty room."

"Yeah, right." Kilbraide didn't want to say it, but he was stunned at her answer. "You knew about it?"

"It was a strange twist to our country's war on drugs."

Kilbraide studied her. "Who are you?"

"You saw my badge."

"Oh, come on." He didn't like the games. "It's obvious you're not really NIA. CIA? No. Some other combination of the alphabet? I don't know."

"I like being upfront, so I'm direct when I need to be and must be. But as I said, everything is on a need to know and some things you don't need to know. I'll be honest about it. It's for your own protection that you're kept in the dark."

"Well, that certainly makes me feel good."

"Detective, to ease your mind, let's just say we're a Dark Op, operating independently, but under the banner and, sometimes, the direction of the NIA."

"Oh great. So counter-terrorism, espionage, and secret spy stuff?"

"Call it what you will."

"Look Agent Catalonia, as much as I want to see Stevens behind bars for the rest of his life, I don't want to be here, like this."

"You don't have a choice in the matter. If you're not going to cooperate with us voluntarily, then I'll reinstate your Army commission and order you to do your duty."

"Wow. I guess you should reinstate me then. With hazard pay I assume."

"You'll be compensated."

"Great. Can we move on then?" Kilbraide quizzed her. "What do you mean the 'war on drugs.'?"

"We can agree that cocaine, fentanyl, opioids are terrible addictions, right?"

"Yeah."

"Hurts our people and, ultimately, hurts the U.S.," said Catalonia. "But more than that, the money made off the sales fuels international arms sales and terrorist groups—who can do the bidding for folks like the Evil Triad of Iran, North Korea, and Venezuela. Don't forget China. And the drug lords in Colombia, Mexico. And the list goes on."

"Okay. I'm still following you. Common knowledge, nothing classified about that."

"Stevens acted like a lone soldier, taking out the people who financed huge sums of drugs. Made sense, too, since it tied into his personal revenge for his wife dying of an overdose. But Stevens is just an operative, one of the world's top snipers being used to eliminate targets and instill fear in others. Quite a strategy, though incredibly risky."

"It sounds like you already know everything about Stevens."

Catalonia was matter of fact. "We know everything about Stevens—complete file from birth through—well, right up until the time you shot him and he disappeared from the hospital. He vanished off our radar and has just recently resurfaced. He's SOG, Special Operations Group, but not CIA. He's contracted with Black Eagle and—"

"Black Eagle? Is that supposed to mean something to me?"

"They're a deep Black Ops. Really high up in the food chain. Top-level. Untouchable. Unlimited resources, and definitely people you don't want to fuck with."

"This is just getting better by the moment." Kilbraide rubbed his temples. "My head's spinning here. Let me get this straight. You're NIA, but not really, just some type of Black Ops?"

Catalonia didn't respond, so Kilbraide continued. "Dark ops, as you said, secret government ops, or whatever you want to call it, and there's all these other clandestine Black Ops? And Stevens is working for this Black Eagle and the U.S. government has no control over what the hell they're doing?"

"To simplify it, yes."

"And you're all working for the good of America?"

"We like to think so. Black Eagle has their agenda, their orders, but different means and different motives for accomplishing them. We're all on the same side, but somebody over there has crossed the line with this one, and it's our job to terminate their Kill Order."

"Get the government to stop them."

"We are the government."

"So, do you have some cool secret code name like Black Eagle."

"We do. Vanguard."

"Vanguard? That's it?"

"Yeah. Short and sweet. Would it make you feel better if we put black in there. We could be Black Vanguard."

"Cute. It's not the name. It's what happening that concerns me."

"Like what?"

"Let's talk about what happened in LA. Something I know about."

"Okay."

"You're telling me that you knew Stevens was murdering people, the drug kingpins, and you didn't do anything about it?"

"We didn't intervene because, well, he was doing a service for the good of the country, protecting our foreign interests. And now, this time, we agree again with his handlers, Black Eagle, that the people he's targeting are detrimental to the fabric of our Constitution, but we disagree with the method—drug dealers are one thing, but public officials and well-known personalities are another. He's crossed the line because these assassinations are not the preferred method for taking back control of our country. In fact, the killings could have unforeseen consequences."

"I see. So who're the good guys?"

"We are. Of course."

"And what assurance do I have of that?"

"The assurance of the U.S. government. And your mission right now is to do what you do best—take out Bob Stevens. A kill shot. That's your only concern. Is that clear, Captain Kilbraide?"

"Captain? No promotion?"

"No."

"Alrighty then. I guess my commission's officially reinstated."

"It is."

Kilbraide nodded. He felt the jet dip and saw the flaps adjust on the wings. Out the window were jagged peaks with patches of snow. The Rockies. The jet dipped again. He figured they were only minutes from landing.

CHAPTER NINE

Uneasiness crept like an unwelcome guest, as though it had followed Bob Stevens along the road, through the thick forests of the Santa Cruz Mountains, and stepped inside with him as he opened the door to his cabin. He boiled water for peppermint tea, but the gnawing was stubborn. Reality was a bitch. Stevens was the best at what he did, but now, for some reason, he felt uneasy and didn't like what he was ordered to do. It's his job—*save America.* He agreed that the targets he was taking out were a threat to the country he loved, but for the first time in his career, he had doubts about the method.

One of the most flamboyant persons to ever have the title of U.S. senator was dead along with one of the richest men in the world. Stevens could hide from the law, he could even bug out from society, but he couldn't run away from his doubts. The killings in Los Angeles weren't the same. He took revenge for the death of his wife, a drug overdose, and he didn't care what happened if he had gotten caught. But now....

Julius Brae and Alanasian were intent on selling out the United States and eliminating the freedoms, the rights, and the national security he had fought so hard to achieve in the Marines. But once he pulled the trigger on the idiot senator, he knew that this was different.

In LA, he didn't care if he had died. But now, he wanted to live. Amanda was not only walking into his life, but was also walking up the steps to his porch. She knocked.

"Just a second." He made his way quickly and opened the door. "Hey."

She smiled. "Hi, Bob. I thought that was your truck. You left a hammer and pliers at my place. I figure I better give them back if I need you to work on the chicken coop again."

"Thanks." He suddenly felt lighter as he took the tools.

"I made beef stew and was wondering if you'd like to come by for dinner. I made a berry pie for dessert." She emphasized dessert with a smile.

Stevens' phone vibrated on a table near the doorway. "Uh, yeah. Just a second." He set the tools down and grabbed the phone. His eyes widened as he read the text.

"But you're busy?" Amanda sounded disappointed.

"No. But I got to return this."

"I could have texted you, but I was out for a walk—"

"That's fine, Amanda. I'd appreciate it. Stopping by for dinner, I mean." He glanced at his phone and then absent-mindedly at the clock in the hallway, as though his phone didn't have the correct time.

"In about an hour?"

He set his phone aside. "Yeah, sure. Sounds good. I'll see you then. At your place?" *Stupid question.*

She laughed. "Yes, my place."

He smiled. "Okay. Thanks. Want me to bring anything?"

"Don't worry. I've got it covered. Unless you don't like stew or don't eat meat."

"Oh, no. I eat meat all right."

"Okay. You're always welcome to bring your own dish as a back-up," she joked.

He relaxed. "I'm more than happy to try your cooking."

"Okay, so see you in a little bit?"

"You got it."

His phone vibrated again.

It caught Amanda's attention. "Better get that, hmm?"

"Yeah. A pesky client but it's no big deal."

"Okay. I'll set the table for two." She waved and walked away.

Stevens took the phone and read the cryptic messages. *Confirm.* He sent a text in reply. *I'm here.*

Instructions came within seconds. *You fly tonight. Midnight.*

Stevens never questioned them, but this time he needed answers.

Where?

There was a long pause before they responded. *Instructions to follow. One hour.*

Amanda would be enjoying small talk with him about that time, but he didn't have a choice. *Acknowledged.*

That was the life of a secret soldier—someone who had vowed to serve his country at all costs and setting his personal comfort, and feelings, aside to carry out a mission. The discipline included focusing on one target at a time and not trying to second guess the long-term result or wonder if America would be better off. His ability to make surgical strikes was absolutely necessary. He would do his duty and follow his orders.

And just as important was his ability to not get entangled in any emotional attachments—professional or personal.

CHAPTER TEN

Kilbraide glanced at the twin bed and poked his head in the closet-sized bathroom with a basic toilet, sink, and shower. "So, I won't be touring the Rocky Mountains?"

"Only if you're hunting for Stevens," said Catalonia.

The room was government issue cinder block, off-white. A lamp and nightstand were near the bed along with a pad of paper, pen, and basic laptop.

"I bookmarked some research material for you." Catalonia pointed to the computer. "Look it over and get caught up to speed."

This wasn't a Marriot or even a Holiday Inn Express.

"Can I get YouTube or, hey, Instagram?"

"No."

Kilbraide felt like he was in a jail cell. "You sure I'm not a prisoner?"

"No, you're not."

He smirked. "You guys spend all that money on a fancy jet to bring me all the way here, and these are the accommodations?" He looked at the bed. "There's not enough room to turn over on that. Hell, boot camp was nicer."

Catalonia acted annoyed. "Get settled. In an hour meet me in the conference room, it's down the hall. We'll lay out an initial strategy. At least we're giving you dinner."

"That's good to hear. Hopefully it's something I like."

"A step above MREs." She didn't crack a smile. "I'm relying on you, Kilbraide. I argued strongly for bringing you into this so don't let me down." Catalonia locked eyes with him but didn't wait for a reply as she left.

Argued strongly? With who? Who is she answering to?

The Bob Stevens case must have been followed closely. What do they actually know about the guy? Not just his record, but about him personally. *Hell, what do they know about me?* Kilbraide figured his record as a sniper and his military career was thoroughly combed through.

Get settled? He laughed. He had no clothes to unpack and no place to sit, other than the narrow bed. No TV. Not even a radio. Claustrophobia could settle in if he let it. But his mind was working without any distractions and that was the goal of his minimalist quarters. A pad, a pen, and a cheap laptop. So that was the game. This was a barebones approach to fighting a war.

As far as the U.S. government was concerned, or for someone in the government, the once-Detective Brian Kilbraide was deemed important enough to be reinstated as a captain in the Army and had to hunt down an enemy—on American soil. One lone warrior hunting another.

Kilbraide plopped on the bed, picked up the computer, and scrolled through all the specifics that Catalonia marked. *Interesting insights.* He glanced at the pen and paper. His mind was revving up. He grabbed the pen, opened the pad, turned it horizontal on his lap, and marked the lower left margin, *Los Angeles.* And then he wrote down the dates of each shooting.

Above that he drew a circle for the Bay Area and scribbled *Silicon Valley.*

The people who were assassinated in LA had lots of money, but their wealth was made in fairly traditional ways with partnerships in films and television and companies specializing in logistics. One of the victims was an attorney handling finances. Another was a global shipping mogul. Each of the victims shot dead were wealthy and powerful, but they weren't well-known outside of business circles or the Los Angeles social scene. But they all had one thing in common—the drug trade.

The two recent killings were completely different.

People in the U.S. knew more about Julius Brae than they did the President of the United States. And Senator Alanasian was constantly on every talk show, had write-ups in places like *People* magazine, and had his own bestselling book, *Keys to Living the Good Life.* Looks like he overlooked a key detail about knowing one's enemies.

Kilbraide wondered about connections between Brae and Alanasian.

They ran in the same circles, but did they know each other? Did they champion any causes together?

He kept reading and finally looked at the clock. Time to go.

He walked the cinder block corridor toward the main door that he and Catalonia entered through. His footsteps echoed. The place was clean and quiet like a hotel, but without any guests. Catalonia called out.

"In here."

Kilbraide stepped into a stark conference room. Flat-screen monitors showing various locations around the globe covered one wall. A platter of beef and plenty of vegetables was spread out on a table. Water and juice were available to drink. Catalonia sat at the head of the table, a laptop in front of her.

"No soda?" he asked.

"You like soda, don't you?"

Kilbraide smiled. "No, I really don't. It's just nice to have when I'm traveling. Makes everything more special that way. Plus, it makes me burp and settles my stomach."

"Attractive. But you'll have to wait until you're on vacation."

"What trip could possibly top this one?"

"Sit down, Kilbraide, we've got work to do." He slid into a chair and eyed the food. Catalonia powered up her laptop, helped herself to dinner, and laid out the situation. "We're being recorded, just so you're aware."

Kilbraide noticed the multiple cameras. "So how many others are working with us? Or should I ask, working with you? Or, to be even more specific, working for you?"

"That's not your concern."

He scooped up a plate, poured juice and nodded. "So, I've only got one concern, don't I?"

"That's right."

"And you want me focused on him like a hound chasing a fox."

"I'm against fox hunting, it's cruel. But if you want to think of it that way—"

"So why are we here? At this location?" asked Kilbraide.

"This is the brain center of Vanguard and it's convenient. Because from here, we're within a two-hour flight to most of the country. Nimble."

"What if he's still near the Bay Area?"

"He may be."

Kilbraide had an idea. "Then I'll tell you why you didn't let me stay there."

"Go ahead."

"Because he's thinking globally, not locally. Stevens took out a world-renowned public figure, Brae, and a well-known senator who always seemed a little crazy to me. In the past, Stevens picked off drug money people, and now, a tech guru and a policy guy."

"Policy?" Catalonia asked in surprise. "Alanasian's been trying to dismantle our military for years. Remember how he said the U.S. military did nothing more than protect our wealth like junkyard dogs protect old cars?"

"I missed that one." Kilbraide took a bite of the beef. "This is actually pretty good."

"He made a lot of people angry. He always did. It played well in the Bay Area and in enough of California to get him elected, but it pissed off a bunch of other people."

"You mean like Stevens and Black Eagle?"

"That's part of the big picture," said Catalonia.

"Well, there is one connection between the victims. According to that crap you had me read, Brae financed the Free People, Free World conference last year."

"Yes, at a resort in Bali, with Alanasian as the keynote speaker. Every bleeding heart in the world attended, enjoying total luxury while talking about helping the oppressed and underprivileged." Catalonia tapped on the keyboard and referred to one of the monitors on the wall. "I'm going to show you something." She pulled up a map of the U.S. with red, green, and blue lights glowing.

"Looks like Christmas," said Kilbraide, taking another bite and chasing it with water.

"The lights are indicators. In just the past few hours, we've documented influential people who have spoken negatively about the United States. Some are vocal on social media with thousands, or even millions of followers, while others have given speeches trying to change U.S. policy and diminish our rights as free citizens. They're leaders in technology, academia, and business."

"What do the different colored lights mean?"

Catalonia hit a few keys and only the red lights were visible. "These are policymakers. Notice how D.C. is lit up, but so are the state capitols. Green highlights the technocrats."

The most important tech cities were glowing: From New York and Boston; south to Athens, Georgia, and up and down the west coast.

"These areas have active technology hubs with companies working robotics, electronics, and of course, social media," said Catalonia. "Now, watch when I hit blue."

Suddenly, the locations of universities and colleges popped up across the country.

Kilbraide was impressed, but perplexed. "That's a lot of information to digest and a lot of ground to cover."

He surveyed the empty chairs. "I mean, is it just me, or don't we have a team? Or maybe you should hire Santa Claus. He gets around quickly."

"Who says he's not on the payroll?" Catalonia ate slowly and kept a straight face.

Wow, she actually joked. Kilbraide smirked. *Or did she?*

Catalonia continued. "With all this information, we're trying to piece together Steven's next move. We're still combing through remarks and interviews of CEOs, celebrities, and other influencers to include in our database. If we see an overlap of red, green, and blue then that's an area we have to anticipate where Stevens might surface."

"That's it? You're basing his next hit on three points of light?"

"We're also monitoring social media for those who have donated to causes that Brae and Alanasian got behind. People who are high profile and anyone else who's spoken out against America right now."

"You mean like every leftist in Congress, every news personality, and every tech giant? That's a big list of people to try and protect."

"It's our job.

"Oh, and what about Los Angeles?"

"What about it?" asked Catalonia.

"Hollywood. Lots of movie stars and sports heroes there don't like America and they think their opinion matters."

"Yeah, but they just do a lot of talking. There's not much action. It's possible he could strike there again but right now we don't think so."

"*We*?"

"Yep. We have a whole team dedicated to this. You'll get to meet a few people tomorrow and handle some of the equipment you'll have access to."

"And my weapon? I prefer to use my own."

"Sorry. Company issue only. No worries. We have nothing but the best and you'll have everything you need. Weapons, communication, and surveillance gear. And, we have the very latest in drone technology."

"Drones? Do I get to play with them?"

"They're not toys. You'll learn how to use them. Useful tools."

"My tech learning curve is a bit slow. It's simple. Tell me where to acquire my target and I'll take him out for you."

"That's the issue. Even with our network of surveillance, and contacts in the FBI, CIA, and even local police agencies, we don't know where he is. Our challenge is to be ready at a moment's notice."

Kilbraide frowned. "I got another question. Pretty important."

"What is it?"

"Can I get some toiletries like a toothbrush and toothpaste? And deodorant. There's nothing in that room."

"I'm sure we can work something out." Catalonia smiled.

CHAPTER ELEVEN

Stevens watched a video on YouTube of Marcia Schallum signing her book outside the SunRise America studio window in Times Square while munching on leftover stew that Amanda sent home with him. Schallum was a political commentator with a national fanbase who didn't just lean left but embodied progressive values and ideals. A lesser-known colleague interviewed her during the signing. She was disheartened about the recent killings but sounded determined to speak up for peace.

"What we've seen happen is tragic. Brae and Alanasian were two brilliant men who wanted nothing more than peace in the global community and they were murdered for their beliefs."

Readers who eagerly bought her book, *The Right has No Might*, waited patiently for her to autograph the front cover.

"Have we lost our ability in this country to have debates without bloodshed?" The interviewer looked worried.

"Honestly, I hope not. The U.S. must become a player for peace if we want to remain relevant on the global stage." Schallum sighed with dismay as she signed one copy after another. "It's what I write about in chapter four. Civil debate means you have to give up your violent desires. And the Right continually supports violence at every opportunity. We see right-wing ideology that's behind the killings of Julius Brae and my dear friend Senator Alanasian."

Stevens took another bite of stew and scoffed at the remark. *Yeah, right.* Privately, Schallum couldn't stand Alanasian even with his leftist positions. But she hated conservatives even more and raked them over the coals for not supporting abortion rights and putting their own needs above the needs of the working class. Schallum had no interest in a bi-partisan America.

Her pulpit was SunRise America, where she passionately preached that states' rights and representative government had to be "ripped apart" and "the memories be used to decorate the graves of the patriarchy."

Her shrill, rhetorical outbursts at political gatherings and women's conventions led to wild applause and standing ovations, but they didn't come with any particular solutions. That didn't matter to her. Because Alanasian had a huge following and political clout, she had him join her on a stage at a recent Women for Global Governance seminar in the Bay Area where they played to the emotions of suburban women.

Stevens paused the video clip and studied the background. Schallum was sitting outside for this portion of the telecast, but normally she would sit inside with her seat angled near the northern end of the window.

He studied the surrounding areas of Times Square, a place he had recently traveled to as a "tourist."

The orders were set. *Take her out.* The details of scouting around New York City were still being arranged. Black Eagle kept their footprint as small as possible, so they contracted Stevens years ago as an independent operator. It was clear that he had to leave the cabin. Not just for this assignment, but maybe permanently.

He cursed his ever-so-slight hesitation about packing up and taking off.

The reason was that the dinner with Amanda was more than a meal. She smiled, talked about her childhood along the coast and how she loved the mountains but couldn't grow the flowers that she liked because of the local climate. Everything has trade-offs, she said.

She was certainly right about that. One more dinner with her or time spent fixing her chicken coop would become too comfortable. Stevens wasn't in the line of work where he had a choice in the matter. The next assignment was sanctioned and now it was his job to get to mid-town Manhattan and eliminate the target. He had to drive his truck a few hours southeast to the desert and catch a plane that was waiting.

He grabbed his travel bag and gear that was always on the ready and tossed it into his truck where he always felt safe. It was nondescript. If any surveillance cameras had somehow caught the movement of him, or his truck around the parking garage in the Bay Area, it would take hours for a team to filter through the footage, then try and pick him out and connect the dots.

There was one last search through the cabin. If he failed in his mission, then the place would get scrubbed. He moved from room to room, thinking about the intel from Black Eagle that Kilbraide was now contracted with Vanguard. Stevens smiled, wondering how Kilbraide felt trailing him instead of fighting crime in LA.

Damn, he'd like to work with him. When he first read an interview that Kilbraide gave in *Military Today* he was impressed with the man's personal discipline and how he took a deep dive into the strategy, history, and economics of the region he was fighting in. He knew the personal stories of the local people and understood their mindset. He was good at building relationships and those skills, combined with his knowledge and military training, helped him get into the psyche of the enemy. That way, he did his job quickly and efficiently.

Kilbraide was a true patriot and loved America as much as Stevens—and the fact that they were both Black men meant that they had a connection and a common background. If they worked together then they could help lead the United States to be the constitutional republic it was meant to be, where citizens would flourish and prosper without oppressive interference from the government. That also meant getting rid of narcissistic idiots like Schallum who said a lot, but her words and her idiotic promises of reform were nothing but inflammatory rhetoric to placate the Left and cause division with the Right. She was worse than Alanasian. Her motive for speaking out crazily, like bashing white privilege while dating a White woman who came from a wealthy family, did nothing but boost her ratings. The speaking fees she commanded were outrageous.

Picking her off while tourists watched and traffic crawled by would be satisfying and glorious.

The assignment included Stevens taking the time he needed to get comfortable and choose the angle that worked best. Shooting specific targets without collateral damage showed that those specific individuals were enemies of freedom and liberty. Unlike going after groups like BLM and Antifa that were simply cauldrons of hate spilling into the streets. There were plenty of others who could battle them.

Stevens grabbed another backpack, turned out the lights, closed the front door, and walked through the dark to the truck. He realized that he didn't know where Amanda stood on the issues of the day, but while thinking about her gaze, he also realized something else—it didn't matter.

The thought struck him as his phone buzzed. Another text message. Now what did they want?

But it wasn't them.

Just FYI. You were a fun dinner guest. Bigg Huggz, Amanda.

A smile crossed his face. Fighting for freedom and liberty was getting tougher by the moment.

CHAPTER TWELVE

Kilbraide stood outside on the grounds of the sprawling Vanguard compound and was amazed by the power of the drone he was piloting, as he followed its movements on a monitor. It hovered a few hundred yards and then shot off in one direction, dipped, rose again, and flew back to its original position, keeping the onboard camera steady throughout its short flight.

"These things keep improving," he said, moving the controls on his smartphone's screen. He had watched demonstrations given to the LAPD, but the continued refinements made the drones more stable and faster than ever. The cameras were incredibly powerful.

"By the minute it seems," said Catalonia.

Kilbraide made one last maneuver. He flew it around Catalonia's back and caught a glimpse of her butt before bringing the drone lower and clicked a button. He struggled to keep a straight face.

Catalonia gave him a dirty look. "Once we find Stevens, this is how we'll follow him."

"This tech stuff is cool," said Kilbraide. "But I don't see the point. It only seems useful if we already know the area the target will be in and then it gives us another eye in the sky. Plus, it takes manpower and resources to keep it airborne."

The camera locked onto her again and kept her in view.

"Really?" She rolled her eyes.

"Just practicing." Kilbraide shrugged.

She revealed more of how the strategy would work. "We have dozens of these in areas where Stevens could likely strike next. They're semi-autonomous, flying around looking for their pre-programmed targets using facial recognition and returning to docking stations for repairs and re-charging."

"That's scary," remarked Kilbraide.

"You don't know the half of it." Catalonia continued. "The most recent images that we have of Stevens have been loaded into a cloud-based repository. The drones are programmed to update when newer images come across."

Kilbraide figured that escaping the long arm of the law was soon going to be impossible for anyone. He was puzzled. "Hey, I'm curious. When I take him out, then what'll you tell all those hungry journalists aching to tell the public about the manhunt underway?"

"If all goes according to plan, we'll have a clean-up crew scrub the scene, leaving no trace of Stevens and who he was, or his history. And as far as what the public will know, the killer will die from a self-inflicted gunshot wound after a stand-off in some remote location." Catalonia continued before Kilbraide could interrupt. "Before you say anything, no, he'll not be connected back to the assassinations in LA that you were investigating. We'll paint him as a copycat killer, some rightwing nut-job."

"That's good. I don't want to become a celebrity and write a bestselling memoir," said Kilbraide.

Catalonia ignored him and checked messages rolling in on her phone. "We have a strategy session in thirty."

"Again?"

"Yeah. Go get ready." She hurried off to the building.

Kilbraide watched her walk away until she disappeared inside.

He hit a button and the drone flew off to its docking station. "That's a good boy."

He figured he should have said that he'd like to marry her some day and see if the comment changed her poker face. He went to his room to freshen up, shower, and maybe catch twenty winks.

So where could he use the drone? How would he use it?

He mulled the questions over and laid down but couldn't sleep. Before he knew it, it was time to get busy again so he made his way through the maze of corridors.

In the conference room were several techs tapping away on keyboards and poring through data.

Catalonia was already seated and analyzing results. "The crazies are out in force. The confessions keep flooding in. Listen to this:

I've always hated social media. It's not good for America, so I spent days at the rifle range practicing. No one noticed me later as I stood in the parking lot and blasted a hole in the founder of ProfileScene.

"Idiots," remarked Kilbraide. "Someone should tell him that if you stand in the parking lot, it'd be an impossible shot. Unless your bullet can fly around corners."

"We're actually working on that."

"I don't even want to know."

"Good. Because it's not part of your need-to-know list." Catalonia kept reading from the screen. "And the tips keep coming, too. Someone saw an elderly woman hurry from the train near Alanasian's office and she was clutching a handbag. Really helpful."

"Any Sasquatch sightings included?"

"Yes, if you want to know the truth. Along with Chupacabra and the Jersey Devil, we've been getting sightings again of the Block Ness Monster in Rhode Island."

"Block Ness? Someone's got a sense of humor." Kilbraide glanced at the interactive map on the wall. "The lights are glowing nicely."

Seattle and south-central Texas were especially lit up.

Catalonia scanned her laptop. "You ever been to Austin?"

"Nope."

"You're going there."

"Really? I was just feeling settled. Thanks for the toothpaste, by the way."

"You're welcome. Now, focus. There's a conference happening and one of the speakers is Dr. George Elias, a leading robotics researcher."

"Okay."

"He knew Julius Brae fairly well and he's made some inflammatory remarks about how robots can finally bring about a fair and just society."

"You mean the guaranteed income debate?"

"Exactly. Except that he's calling for an end to capitalism as we know it."

"Capitalism? Who cares? I work for the government."

Catalonia was annoyed. "Cut the crap, Kilbraide."

"Gallows humor, okay?"

"I get it. Look at this. He's speaking at an outdoor pavilion, downtown, near 6th Street. The whole area is being blocked off for the conference."

"And you think Stevens will show up? Or show up in the shadows, as he has done."

"Damned good possibility. There's a demonstration planned to coincide with Elias' speech. Right-wing groups are coming out of the woodwork."

"Like the Proud Boys?"

"Could be. We're picking up the chatter."

"They're afraid that robots will take away jobs, I'll bet."

"They're afraid of losing America."

"Although people need to be hired to service the robots," mused Kilbraide.

Catalonia raised an eyebrow. "Sorry, I'm a bit too preoccupied and could care less about the jobs-robots debate. Antifa is planning a counterdemonstration."

"Sounds like a brawl is brewing."

"The police are going to have everyone available. A greater police presence, but that also means lots of distractions to provide cover for Stevens."

"Isn't the stage going to be protected?" asked Kilbraide. But then he thought of the weapon used to take out Brae and Alanasian. "Although Dr. Elias would need to be in a bomb shelter."

"That's about it."

"Have they thought about moving the event indoors?"

"Elias has said he's not scared of his haters. And moving the venue would only make him look weak. And if he is assassinated, he'll just become a martyr and his cause will still continue."

"How are you so sure Stevens will strike in Austin? Aren't there other conferences happening?" He looked over at the glowing lights on the map. "Looks to me like there are targets everywhere."

"This is high profile," said Catalonia. "If another person with a national reputation gets killed then that would send a signal that differing political views won't be tolerated."

Kilbraide smiled. "So, are you going to fly with me on the jet? Just the two of us?" He gave her a sexy wink.

She groaned. "You're a big boy. You can fly alone. Or alone with a team of techs watching your back."

"You know, I've been thinking about this. What if I refuse?"

"You won't. You'll do your duty, Captain Kilbraide."

"Oh? But what if I don't?"

Catalonia didn't flinch. "You'll get *disappeared*."

"Are you serious?"

"Deadly."

"I guess I'm going to Austin, then."

"Yes. You need to start prepping. Learn every possible hide in and around the downtown area. Find yourself a good one, get an eye on Stevens, and shut him down."

CHAPTER THIRTEEN

One person after another laid their keys, wallets, and anything else in their pockets on the conveyor belt and walked through the metal detector. The line moved slowly and steadily as fans made their way in for a studio tour of SunRise America under the watchful eyes of security. People who passed through moved excitedly into a spacious lobby and were greeted by a staff member.

Stevens was next. He was aware of the security cameras and eyed the other people in the group who he could stand behind to help obscure his face.

"Everything out of the pockets, sir," said the security guard, sounding bored, and motioning to the basket.

Stevens pulled out keys and his pen.

The bucket started along the belt and passed through the screening device while Stevens walked through the metal detector. *Buzz.*

"Anything in your pockets?" asked another guard.

"Uh," he reached in one pocket and then another. "Yeah, just a quarter."

One of the guards pulled out a metal detector wand. "Lift your arms."

Stevens did as directed and the security guard ran the wand over his arms, around his back pockets, and along his thighs. When the wand got too near his groin, Stevens silently groaned that this isn't the America that he grew up in where kids said the pledge of allegiance with a sense of patriotism. Nobody trusts anybody, any longer.

Satisfied, the guard waved him on to join the rest of the group.

Inside the lobby, he waited with men and women in a reception area. Paneling covered one part of a wall and Stevens guessed that on the other side was where the production took place for Marcia Schallum and the rest of the SunRise America hosts.

Some of the people had children. He hated how they looked—smiling and dancing around eagerly. So, they were going to tour a TV studio. But they couldn't tell how badly the information from this show and others like it was damaging their own lives. They were like rats being led into a trap.

A staff member, a woman in a blue blazer and neatly pressed slacks, welcomed the group, gave a brief history of the network, and motioned for them to follow her down a hallway. They passed elevator doors and the guide explained about the most famous personalities who worked for the network and how SunRise America got its start.

What Stevens noticed was how she batted her eyes with the men in the group and he wondered how long it would be before she filed a false claim, suing one of the network execs for sexual harassment just because he smiled at her in passing.

He hated politically correct culture and how extreme PC had become, and how so many *victims* reaped rewards at the expense of others. But he couldn't be sidetracked from his mission—

"Sir. Excuse me, sir." It was the guide calling to him from farther down the corridor.

He had gotten lost in his thoughts.

"Looks like someone is a bit starstruck," quipped the tour guide while the crowd chuckled. "That's understandable since this studio is filled with some of broadcasting's most iconic names."

Stevens hurried to catch the group as they turned around one corner and then another.

Dressing rooms were on the left. The lobby was on the opposite side of the wall. And the studio was on the right of the group. The walls were glass and gave a full view of the cameras and where the anchors were seated while on air.

The guide mentioned the show had already finished shooting for that morning, but they were still to be quiet as they entered the studio. She opened the door and stepped in. In one corner, a few of the show's personnel were discussing that morning's broadcast.

Stevens caught a sense of the ceiling's height and where the cameras were stationed and did his best to stay in the middle of the group. He noticed the positioning of the craft services' table, on-set makeup, and wardrobe areas. He grasped every detail and committed the layout to memory. He looked over to where Schallum would be sitting and traced a line of sight across the studio.

On the far side, exterior windows gave a full view of the busy New York City street outside. The sidewalk was a spot where passersby, mostly tourists, could watch the taping of the show through the bullet-proof windows. Correction, thought Stevens. No window is truly bulletproof, only bullet resistant.

He glanced outside to get a full view of the street as the guide droned on.

What was across the street? What locations gave clear lines of sight into the studio? And then he had an idea. And though it was cliché, it might actually work. A delivery truck with a small hole drilled in the side, parked near a manhole. One damned good shot, slither out of the truck and—no, that's straight fantasy out of a Hollywood movie.

Suddenly, a woman's voice that had a nasal tone rang out from the corner. "Welcome, folks. Come on over and say hello."

The small group in the far corner parted and there she was—Martha Schallum in the flesh.

"Well, this is a surprise," said the guide, twisting so quickly she looked like she'd break her neck.

"Come on over." Schallum was all smiles. "I've even got a few copies of my book. Who'd like one?"

Get rid of the books any way you can, mused Stevens. He wasn't sure if this was a bonus, or torture.

"Let's shake hands and be friends," said Schallum, "even if you're a Republican."

Laughter bounced from the tourists.

Definitely torture, thought Stevens.

She held up a book. "Who wants a copy? They're free. One per family."

Her book sales had taken off the first few days and then plummeted the next week, Stevens noticed during his research.

People in the crowd each accepted one, shook Schallum's hand, and introduced themselves. She was quite outgoing and bubbly. Almost a completely different person than the one who blabbered on television. In the moment, she seemed like a woman Stevens could sit down with for a cup of coffee and have a friendly debate about the issues of the day.

"Hello, sir," Schallum looked at Stevens. "Shall I autograph one for you?"

His hands suddenly felt like cement and his mouth was dry. "Thank you." He knew the cameras were picking him up.

"What's your name?"

Stevens smiled at a sudden inspiration. "Brian. Brian Kilbraide."

"And what brings you to Times Square?"

This was totally unexpected. "Just here on business, maybe have some fun, cause a little trouble."

The crowd fanned out and formed a perimeter around him and the television host.

"I'll put you on the spot. Are you a fan of the show?"

Stevens was stiff but tried to relax. He never had to talk with someone he was about to kill. "I've been watching, well, a short time."

"Good. I hope you continue watching." Schallum was all smiles as she extended a hand.

Stevens smiled and shook her hand. It felt strange touching his target and he held on a little too long for comfort. She gracefully pulled away from his grasp and looked him in the eye.

Schallum laughed. "Earth to Brian."

"Oh, sorry. Sure. I will. Uh, I do have one question."

"Yes?"

"Do you always sit in the same spot?"

In that moment, he studied her face—how close her eyes were together and how the bridge of her nose formed. Her jawline was relaxed, and her smile was wide.

She laughed. "That's the first time I've been asked that. Well, yeah, most of the time. Besides SunRise America, what's your favorite news show?"

"I flip through so many of them that I simply don't have a favorite."

"So, the news flips you out?" Schallum and the crowd laughed.

Stevens was amused and annoyed by the conversation. "There's so much of it. And you don't know who's telling the truth. What's fake? What's real?"

"Ah, a skeptic. That's why I'm here and why SunRise America is on the air."

The woman was a sales pro.

"Why?" Stevens snarky side jumped out.

For a second, Schallum was annoyed with a flash of anger, but she recovered. "For the truth."

"I see." Stevens was quiet and felt he was almost too quiet. A security guard in one corner of the room must have sensed tension. Awkwardly, Stevens reached for the book. "Okay, thank you for greeting us."

But Schallum held it firm. "Anything special you'd like me to write?" She held her pen at an angle.

The guard started over, but Schallum waved him off.

"I'm just a bit nervous. I've never met a celebrity before."

Schallum laughed and proclaimed to the crowd. "You might watch me and read my books, but I'll assure you one thing."

"What's that?"

"We need to learn to get along. We're all in this crazy life together."

"And it's over before you know it," mumbled Stevens.

"We strive for the truth, and that's the truth." Schallum smiled, opened the book, and signed the inside front cover. *To Brian. Life is short. Do what you can to make this world a better place.*

"Thank you." Stevens took the book and stepped back into the gathering as just another unimportant face in the crowd.

CHAPTER FOURTEEN

Kilbraide's dark sunglasses filtered the Texas sun, but also enhanced the clarity of things hidden in the shadows of the buildings. He carried a small backpack with some gear and a tablet for downloading messages and data from Catalonia's security team. Images were being captured and processed through facial recognition from the Austin International Airport, regional airports, the downtown area, and points around the state capitol. But there were no leads on Stevens and his whereabouts.

The atmosphere appeared more festive than politically charged since the gathering was meant to coincide with the Pecan festival and commemorate the city's founding. 6th Street in the entertainment district was already packed with tourists and revelers. To add to the chaos, protestors were bussed in from around the country.

Dr. Elias was leading an *automation movement* that would reduce the hours people worked while guaranteeing an acceptable, living wage, and giving more time for leisure and personal development. He saw how robots could bring about a socialist utopia. Elias believed that Austin was the perfect blend of education, arts, technology, and politics to kick off a historical moment that he called *transcendent.*

Whatever that means, thought Kilbraide. He had skimmed through articles that Elias had authored, not to digest the content but to get an idea of how the man interacted with the city.

The speech for Dr. Elias was supposed to be academic and low key, a lecture explaining his positions. He didn't mean for it to be like an emotional campaign speech. He wanted to provoke discussion and debate. Social media users and influencers, though, made sure that a civil discussion was impossible.

Passion and threats online had been building for hours and now the ranks of protestors and counter-protestors were already forming. Riot police were standing guard as Kilbraide walked to a park and readied his drone to fly up and along the streets with the capitol rotunda in the distance. Catalonia made sure the local police knew that a federal investigative agency was surveilling the area.

The ever-popular 6th Street was closed to through traffic to allow the revelers easy access to restaurants, bars, and the array of bands, stand-up comedians and storytellers of all varieties. Kilbraide located the Ideas of Our Time stage, the place where Elias and other innovators would speak.

Militants with rainbow-colored hair, clad in black hoodies, were forming a protective flank around the perimeter where Elias would take the stage. Opposing them was an assembly of men and women dressed in dark T-shirts emblazoned with gold lettering. They were mostly just milling about with occasional shouts back and forth, but Kilbraide figured that since Texas had open carry laws that many would be armed in support of their slogan FAFO: *Fuck Around and Find Out.*

Kilbraide empathized with the Austin PD. The officers were going to have full days and nights keeping the factions from destroying each other and the city in the process. But that was their problem and he was glad that he didn't have to deal with it. Kilbraide flew the drone over the stage and angled the camera to study the surrounding buildings. He tried to picture where a sniper like Stevens would hide out and have a clear line of sight to the podium. The only redeeming factor about Stevens was that he had a surgical approach and took out one target at a time. He'd shown that he wasn't interested in mass casualties and it was amazing, or a gift from God, that innocent bystanders had never been killed in the process. Hard to believe, but Stevens had a moral code—no collateral damage.

Kilbraide retrieved the drone with a good sense of the layout and what he was up against. Catalonia's crew was scanning images from various feeds but apparently there weren't any findings. More shouts came from the demonstrators. A police line moved between them. The anger was going to cost the taxpayers dearly. He figured few people really paid attention to the debates and wondered how many even cared about the death of Julius Brae. ProfileScene was up and running again and for most people across the nation, their access to social media was really all that mattered.

He sighed. It was time to get a beer, review the drone footage, and report to Catalonia.

***

Stevens stood across from the SunRise America Studios looking like a tourist who was holding up his phone and taking pictures. But he was using it as a rangefinder, visually measuring the distances from several different angles. During the previous mornings, he had studied how the pedestrian traffic, delivery trucks, and cars moved past. He didn't care for the city with its chaos and had always tried to avoid it. Once the mission was accomplished then he'd never come back, he vowed. That's when his phone vibrated with a text message from Amanda. She sent a selfie of her eating and wished him a safe return from his travels.

The image weakened him, but he fought to keep his resolve. *Focus.* That was his mantra. *Focus.* Believe in your calling, believe in your abilities. *You're a warrior. You're a patriot. You're a Marine. Semper Fi. Always loyal, always faithful. Oorah.*

The SunRise America studio was located along America Way at the T of an intersection. At the base of the T there was a boutique hotel where he could rent an upper-floor room with an angle allowing him to shoot directly over the heads of onlookers and through the glass. Once he sent the round, egress from the hotel would place him unnoticed on a side street where he could melt into the pandemonium of New York City.

The selfie of Amanda tugged on his emotions. He wanted nothing more than to be there by her side, enjoying a nice dinner. Or a hike through the woods.

Focus.

He mentally wiped away her image and continued planning. Once he left the hotel, then what? Taking the subway could be too much of a risk with surveillance cameras. Busses would be too slow and taxi drivers seem unpredictable. He thought of Amanda again.

Focus. Focus.

And then he overheard a conversation between people who had waited in line to get tickets and be part of the studio audience for the next day. Stevens interrupted. "Excuse me? What'd you say about Marcia Schallum?"

The crowd was dispersing, but a man hung back.

"Said her mother's sick. The show's still on, but she's not going to be on it."

"That's too bad."

"Yeah, we came up from Philly. Disappointing, but that's how it goes."

Stevens checked with the ticket booth. The people confirmed she was taking a leave and heading up north to Saratoga Springs and visit her ailing mother. But she was going to take the time to do a last-minute book signing while there.

Stevens' mind was reeling. It was a small town but busy with tourists and known for horse racing. He had heard about the mineral baths in the state park, and he had done some satellite wagering on thoroughbred racing hosted at the track. It'd almost be easier to get noticed, but there could also be more opportunity to find a good hide to shoot from.

His heart was pounding. Time to adjust and travel. Time to flee New York City, get the fresh air of upstate, and prepare for the task ahead.

CHAPTER FIFTEEN

Kilbraide was half a block away from the Thirsty Eagle bar hoping for a cold, local brew when his phone vibrated. Catalonia was calling. He picked it up. "Freddie's Pizza."

There was hesitation. "Kilbraide?"

"Yeah."

"Cut the shit." Catalonia was angry.

"What side of the bed did you crawl out of? Oh, never mind."

She was to the point. "We have facial recognition of Stevens in Times Square."

"New York? Ugh. When?"

"The system locked onto him about thirty minutes ago. We've confirmed it's him."

"What the hell's he doing there?" asked Kilbraide.

"That's what we're trying to figure out."

"Where was he exactly?"

"Outside the SunRise America TV studio."

"Sightseeing?"

"Reconnoitering," said Catalonia. "We already got a team on the ground and drones in the air."

"Let me guess, you want me in New York."

"The bird's fueled and waiting."

Kilbraide groaned at the cliché.

"Once you're airborne, you'll be briefed and then I expect you'll be on the ground in a couple of hours."

"And when I get there?"

"Easy-peazy. Find Stevens and kill him."

***

The brick buildings with awnings over the windows gave Saratoga Springs a welcoming feel for most visitors. Stevens walked slowly along Basset Street, eyeing the sidewalk and the location of the Turn the Page bookstore, Schallum's favorite that she wrote about in her book. It was one story high with red brick, and the front of the building had two large rectangular windows and a narrow front door. He noticed the plaque on the outside: Registered Historical Site, Built 1859.

People were smaller then. *And tougher, too.*

The storefront window had a display of a large teddy bear wearing wire-rimmed glasses, reading a poetry book. No posters or flyers indicated that Schallum was scheduled for a book signing.

That was the problem with historical buildings. Times had changed and people had grown wider and taller. Soft, in fact, mused Stevens. He checked under the eaves and above the door for security cameras, but he didn't see any and stepped inside.

"Hello, may I help you?" asked a woman, sitting behind a counter laden with ceramic teddy bears, tiny cows, and other knickknacks. She was writing on small sales tags. She sniffled, wiped her red nose, and smiled. She looked mid-twenties.

"Just looking, thank you."

The store was split into three aisles with gifts along both walls and bookshelves down the middle. Stevens strolled down the middle aisle. The back of the store had a wide-open area that was perfect for author readings, and out the back door was a patio covered by shade trees.

Damn. Like many small towns, specialty stores, coffee shops, and other small businesses were often located in what had been residences with small backyards. There was a fence along an alleyway, and beyond the line of shade trees, one-and-two-story buildings filled his vision. It was hard to tell if they were private homes or bed and breakfast businesses.

Challenges began swarming through Stevens' mind. It was always a puzzle and he looked forward to figuring it out as he stepped back inside, bumping elbows with two elderly women wearing extra red lipstick. He went to the front counter.

"Excuse me."

"Yes?" The woman kept writing on the tags and affixing them to the figurines.

"I heard Marcia Schallum was doing a book signing."

"Yes, she is." The woman went back to her work. "Tomorrow."

"Oh, there's no sign in your window."

The woman frowned. "No, there's not. But once we know the time and location then we'll put up a sign. But honestly, all I have to do is post it online and alert a few book clubs in town and they'll take care of the rest."

"Oh, I see." Stevens smiled in return. "What do you mean you don't know the location?"

"It could be here, which, of course, I would love. I'm so looking forward to meeting her. She's such a free-thinker, and I couldn't agree more with her views."

Stevens groaned silently and had to stop himself from rolling his eyes as the woman, *the ill-informed woman*, continued.

"But it may be at the college where she attended as an undergrad." The woman sneezed and then wiped her nose with her sleeve.

Stevens stepped back.

"Oh, sorry. Allergies."

"No problem," he replied. "When will you know about the signing?"

She shrugged. "I'm not sure. Could be later this afternoon."

Stevens laughed. "Very casual, I see."

"This *is* upstate after all. We're pretty laid back. Check our website or follow us on ProfileScene. It'll be posted as soon as we know. Are you a fan, too?"

"Yeah, of a sort. I'm traveling through and I'd hate to miss her."

"Yes," said the woman. "She's very popular." She turned to a few other people entering the store. "Hello, welcome. Let me know if you need help finding things."

"Thank you."

Stevens kept digging. "Definitely. I know it's last minute, but I figured since she's a big celebrity, there'd have to be careful planning."

"Oh, I suppose that would be ideal. But, small town mentality." The woman laughed. "Hey, I lived in Manhattan after college working in publishing."

"Oh, yeah?"

"Yeah. Everything ran like clockwork, every moment of every day. And you know what?"

"What?"

"After a couple of years, the bright lights and big city wore on me. So I gave it up, moved back home and am truly enjoying the good life. Though my dad would prefer that I move out and get a place of my own." She sniffled, glanced around the counter, and found a tissue to wipe her nose. "Damned allergies."

"Thank you for all the information." Stevens was getting annoyed at the useless banter.

"I'll tell you what. Do you have a cell phone? Oh, dumb question." She handed him a business card. "Call me in a couple of hours and I can tell you if the signing will be here or at the college."

"That's very kind of you. If it's at the college, then where would it be?"

"Quill Hall, that's the building that houses the English department. Marcia Schallum studied fiction and journalism there."

"Is that why she makes up stories on current events?" Stevens grinned.

The woman was silent and then laughed. "Oh, I get it. That's very funny. Yes, fiction and journalism do seem to go together these days."

"Unfortunately, yes." Stevens didn't want to waste time trying to set her straight, so he reluctantly agreed with her.

"I believe Marcia Schallum speaks for the truth."

Stevens clenched his jaw and his fists tightened as she continued.

"Did you see that segment on SunRise America the other month where they had the polar bear in the studio and—"

Stevens was feeling antsy. "No, I didn't,"

"Oh. You said you followed her closely."

"As closely as I can. I do a lot of traveling for my work."

"What do you do?"

"Estate planning. I help people think about the afterlife."

The woman furrowed her brow and laughed. "That's such bullshit. There's no afterlife. It's all just here and now. Enjoy it while you can."

Stevens needed to leave but remained polite. "We'll just have to disagree on that."

"Oh, okay Boomer." She laughed. "I'm just playing with ya."

"No problem. And thank you. I'll make sure to check your site." He started to leave.

"By the way, you called her a celebrity. Honestly, I probably shouldn't tell you this," the woman looked around and then spoke quietly again, "but she's just a small-town girl. I mean, she's not even staying in one of the fancy hotels uptown."

"Really?"

"Yeah. She always stays at her mother's over on Grainger Street."

"You mean she's a real person?" Stevens' inflection encouraged the woman to keep talking.

"Definitely. She'll even stand on the porch and wave to people passing by."

"Isn't Grainger Street a few blocks that way?" He motioned.

The woman laughed and pointed in the opposite direction. "It's that way, about three blocks down. Her mother's house is right behind Pike's Coffee and Desserts. She and her mom always have breakfast there. But, maybe not now, since her mother's sick."

"I heard. I hope she's going to be okay."

"Speaking of which—" The woman scrunched her face, reached for a tissue, squinted, and tilted her head back anticipating a sneeze. Stevens didn't wait around and was out the door.

CHAPTER SIXTEEN

The jet circled over New York, descended, touched the runway and suddenly the engines roared back to full power. Kilbraide was rocked side to side, wondered what was happening, and felt the strange pull of motion sickness as the plane climbed above the city and back into the clouds. The pilot spoke to him over the intercom. "Sorry for the touch and go. Change of plans, we're flying north."

Before Kilbraide could respond, his phone vibrated. "Yeah?"

"Scratch New York," said Catalonia, "you're going to Saratoga Springs."

"Okay. Where exactly is that?"

"Upstate. About an hour from Albany. Famous for horse racing, hot springs. Ring a bell?"

"No."

"The colonists had a key victory therc during the Revolutionary War."

"Oh, yeah. 1777. Turning point in the war."

"Oh, so you do know your history?"

"Studied a bit. Care to share what's going on?" asked Kilbraide.

"We believe Stevens is targeting the TV personality Marcia Schallum."

"I can't stand her, either."

"Leave your personal feelings out of it. We just got all the tapes from the SunRise America studio tour yesterday morning and Stevens was there."

"On the tour?"

"Clear as day," said Catalonia. "He kept looking away from the cameras, but we got him from all angles. In fact, he was talking and shaking hands with Schallum."

"That's out of character for him."

"With her audience reach, influence, political views, and hobnobbing with the likes of Brae and Alanasian she's got to be Stevens' next target."

"Why Saratoga?"

"Her mom's ill. She went up there to see her, and of course, being the celebrity that she is, she's going to do a book signing. Promoting her new book."

"Never miss a chance, huh?"

"Her new book that she signed a copy of for Stevens. Apparently, they had a little conversation."

"What? Gets stranger by the second. Does anybody know what they were talking about?"

"Just chit-chat. Nothing that anybody remembers or could pick up. Though one of the security guards got a weird feeling about Stevens. Thought the guy was a little creepy. But just chalked it up to a fan being nervous about meeting a celeb."

"I'll bet he won't wash his hands for a week."

"Funny," she said, sarcastically.

"Not really, I know," said Kilbraide. "So, getting back to business. Do I still have the same orders?"

"You better believe it. We're making arrangements for you to stay at a bed and breakfast. The local P.D. were told to watch Schallum since she's popular, especially in light of what happened to Brae and Alanasian. And, Kilbraide, they don't know anything about you, and we want to keep it that way. Got me?"

"Yeah, I do. I can't get any jaywalking tickets."

"Of course not. Check your devices in the next half hour. We're going to send you a shitload of intel and updates about the area." Catalonia paused. "I can see you'll be landing soon."

"This *bird* makes good time."

"Yep, the fastest."

"Saratoga Springs is pretty small, isn't it?"

"Yeah. About twenty-eight thousand people."

"Is that it?" Kilbraide was thinking. "Any sightings of Stevens? Airports? Car rentals? Anything?"

"Nope. He ghosted, but you'll be the first to know."

"Can I at least watch the ponies run and place some bets at the track?"

"This is the first real lead we've had. We're close. I need your head in the game. Enough with the jokes. Find Stevens and take him out."

"Yes, *Sir.* Head in the game. Check."

"Kilbraide, I'm warning you."

He missed the camaraderie that he had with Stone and Jake in LA. "So this Marcia Schallum is—" Kilbraide stopped in mid-sentence.

Catalonia waited and then responded. "You went silent on me."

"I'm thinking," said Kilbraide. "Like is this going to be easier or harder than if it was in New York City?"

"Unknown. Just get a feel for the town after you land. And think about it. If you were Stevens, where would you take the shot from?"

"Stevens could be anywhere. We've got to figure out where Schallum will be, her schedule, and that's where Stevens will be. So far he's made his kills very public. And hell, that's a problem. He could run up the side of a tree and outfox a squirrel."

"I know. We already have a team working on narrowing down the possibilities."

"That's good to know. Has Schallum been notified? Why not put her in protective custody?"

"Yes, she's been informed. But she has a strong stance on Defund the Police and doesn't want to look like a hypocrite in front of her fans and has refused any protection."

"Dumbass," scoffed Kilbraide.

"Can't argue with you there. She's not making our job any easier. Look, we'll protect her and keep America safe. But you know Stevens and it's your duty to stop him."

"Easy-peazy," said Kilbraide, fighting dizziness as the plane dipped and descended.

***

Stevens stepped outside the grocery store and into his car when a small jet roared on its approach to the county airport. The wealthy often flew in and out with their own jets, so he thought nothing of it as he drove a car that his handlers supplied. His weapon was wrapped up discreetly in the trunk. He slowed to a stop at a traffic light and reached across the seat to tear off a piece of rotisserie chicken before heading to the college. The light turned green, and he wondered a big *What If?*

What if it'd be best to play it safe? Schallum was a vocal idiot, but there were plenty of others like her around the country. Give it time after two major killings.

Why am I doing this? Yeah, to make America safe.

And then he thought about Amanda. She knew he was flying to New York on business but sharing details with her was impossible and he couldn't think of what to make up. Then he wondered how she was doing. He missed her and realized she hadn't sent a selfie in a while. His thoughts were all jumbled. He had to focus. It didn't take long to get to the college. He parked, sent her a text message that he was fine and that he was looking forward to seeing her when he returned. He got out of the car and found the hall.

So where would Schallum be?

Here? Or at the bookstore? And if at the bookstore, would it be inside or out back on the patio?

Stevens had a long afternoon and evening ahead figuring out answers and prepping. Then there was also Schallum's childhood home. It was certainly worth scouting out.

His phone vibrated and his heart raced. *Amanda.* Then his heart sank when he read the text message. It wasn't from her. Black Eagle's intel was working overtime.

Kilbraide landed.

CHAPTER SEVENTEEN

Kilbraide had picked up the car that Catalonia made available for him at the airport. A cheap sub-compact that squished his knees. The drive to the inn was easy, but the clerk made checking in to the Meadow Bed and Breakfast tougher than it should have been. Catalonia assured Kilbraide that all was set and there'd be no questions asked. But the order didn't get passed along.

"And how long do you plan to stay with us?" asked the man, wearing wire-rim glasses with his hair neatly parted in the middle. He looked like he would have fit into the town as a telegraph operator in the 1890s.

Kilbraide glanced at the end of the counter with maps of the town and brochures neatly arranged. "Not certain."

"Your reservation says a week."

Kilbraide hid his surprise and wondered, *Why the hell did you ask?* He took a map of Saratoga. "Yeah, it depends. I may get things done before that."

"Do you golf?"

Kilbraide hated the sport. He thought back to a few weeks earlier when he was at the shooting range. "Don't have the patience for it."

"Do you play the ponies?"

"Love the horses." He wanted to end the chit chat. "But not a gambling man."

"Same. Is there anything in town you'd like to know about?"

The clerk was really trying to be helpful, but, God, he was hitting a nerve again and again. Kilbraide was dying to lie down for a few minutes before scouting the town. "I like history."

"Ahh, there we go. Lots of history in this town. Revolutionary War stuff. Our visitor's center lays out everything about the Battle of Saratoga Springs quite nicely."

"I've read about the battle, so, yeah, that's possible."

"There's a wonderful display of local historical fiction and a bulletin about artifacts at the library."

"I'll check it out if I get a chance," said Kilbraide.

"There's also a great novel at the bookstore, too. *Indomitable Spirit* by Patricia McCormick. Historical fiction. It's about the very colorful woman who founded the Daughters of the American Revolution."

The bookstore.

"How far is that from here?" asked Kilbraide.

"A little over a mile. Just past the center of town, a quiet area." The clerk took a map, scribbled in pen, circling both the bookstore and the library. "Here. It's a great place to relax."

"Thanks for the tip."

"And for dinner tonight?"

This guy didn't quit.

"Who knows? I'll find something, though. Thanks again."

"And, Sir—"

"What?" Kilbraide nearly growled.

"Some items were delivered to your room."

It took all the gibberish to get to the important stuff.

"Thanks."

Fatigue was coursing through Kilbraide as he grabbed the keycard and headed toward his room. The rapid shift in plans and traveling from Colorado to Texas, to New York City, and now upstate was starting to take its toll. A bonus was the quick dip to the runway at La Guardia and then a fast rise into the skies. Kilbraide's stomach was still catching up with him.

He hauled his bag to the second floor. Thanks to Vanguard's PX store, he had grabbed a fresh change of clothes before leaving. His was the last room on the right. Catalonia had texted him that the one next to him would be empty so less chance of being disturbed. Kilbraide sighed. He stayed in great shape, always running, lifting, and eating right. But he needed several minutes to lie down on the bed and close his eyes. And then he'd check the bookstore.

His mind was reeling. Where were all the possible places that Stevens could be hiding out and waiting for Schallum? Hell, this was the guy who lived in a swamp in Los Angeles and then a swamp in the Bay Area to take down his targets. He could be anywhere within a couple of miles.

He scanned the room and opened the closet where Catalonia had delivered his weapon case and surveillance gear. Now for a timeout. He plopped on the bed with its feathery comforter. He wanted to call Stone. The Detective had incredible instincts. Kilbraide took a breath and closed his eyes. Five minutes. Maybe ten minutes, just to stop and clear his mind.

What a strange place for a manhunt.

***

Stevens stood on the expansive lawn, noted the entrance to the English building, and eyed the trees that provided cover around the walkway. *Challenging.* He was trying to visualize how the scene would unfold if Schallum got out of her car and was escorted down the sidewalk. There were options, but almost too many.

He could face the street or the parking lot and when she got out of the car—

But she was supposed to do a book signing. It would be efficient and send a stronger message if he took her out while she was actually signing a book. Where would she be set up? Intel didn't know.

Hopefully, outside with easy access for her fans. But what if she was tucked away inside? He could wait all night and still have no clear shot.

Tension built in his mind and the sweat beads started. How in the hell were Brae and Alanasian so much easier? Was Schallum worth it?

Anger bubbled inside at the uncertainty, but the task also became more appealing. A worthy opponent makes the battle interesting, even though he was struggling. He couldn't reel in his thoughts and it was as though panic was getting the best of him. Something that had never happened before.

And then there was Kilbraide. *What if he was working with me instead of hunting me?*

What if he could talk to him, reason, and tell him that any detective could nab common crooks. Much more was at stake. The future of our country. Kilbraide's a patriot. Served America proudly. He should realize the fact that he could be more than a detective.

How would he talk to him?

Suddenly, Stevens had a brilliant idea. Schallum's book was in the back of his car and he knew just what to do with it.

CHAPTER EIGHTEEN

It was close to 4:00 P.M. as Kilbraide hurried to the bookstore. He'd been in Los Angeles so long that the red brick buildings of a small town in upstate New York seemed foreign. There was a steak house in the historic section that looked great. Maybe grab some dinner there.

Where would Stevens stay in a town like this? The surroundings were quaint and manicured. He was a predator who liked the rough and tumble of decrepit places and desperate people. When Stevens closed in on a victim, he embraced a mindset that blurred reality. His targets had to cease being real people.

One block after another. Kilbraide picked up his pace as he walked under a canopy of trees. He was aching to talk to someone and be part of a real team again. He took out his phone, and dialed. It rang once, twice, three times and then Tom Stone picked up.

"Hello. Stone here."

"Detective Stone, good to hear your voice."

"Kilbraide?"

"Yeah."

"Your name didn't show. I almost didn't pick up."

"Sorry, I'm on a burner. Company issued."

"Makes sense. What's up?"

"I'm missing LA."

"You are? Then things must not be going well."

"Yeah, well, Los Angeles is a city where I have a girlfriend who's starring in films and TV shows."

"You have a girlfriend?" Stone sounded surprised.

"I'm supposed to, right? A man can dream."

Stone laughed. "What can I do for you?"

"Send Marty Brannigan. I need him to put cameras in trees."

"That's not going to happen. He's busy working on a case with me. Uh-hem. Not officially, of course. Besides, I know who the best person is for the job you're on," said Stone.

"Who?"

"Detective Brian Kilbraide. A sharp eye and a keen mind that asks lots of questions."

"Thanks. Right now, I'm wondering where a highly skilled but mentally unstable sniper would hang out."

"Yeah. So what's going on with all that?"

Suddenly, the connection *clicked*, *buzzed*, and went dead.

"Hello, hello? Stone, you there?"

A voice that Kilbraide didn't recognize interrupted. "Detective Kilbraide."

"Yeah, who's this?"

"No unauthorized communication is allowed."

"What? You're monitoring my calls?"

Silence.

"Hey I was homesick, that's all."

Silence.

And then the voice responded. "Detective Stone doesn't have clearance."

Kilbraide mumbled. "Oh, yeah? I'll give you clearance." He clicked off the call and shoved the phone in his pocket, annoyed that he was being monitored.

A few minutes later he reached the bookstore, calmed down, and stepped inside.

"Good afternoon," said the woman behind the counter, wiping her nose with tissue.

"Hi there."

"Let me know if I can help you find anything." She picked up her phone.

"I certainly will." Kilbraide wandered through the store and found it strange that there were no posters or flyers announcing Marcia Schallum and a book signing. He might as well ask so he made his way to the front and waited for the chatty woman to finish her phone call.

Kilbraide feigned interest in a few glass figurines as he listened to the conversation.

"The word at the moment is that she'll be here tomorrow morning just before noon." The woman paused. "I know it's a strange time, but Marcia can't exactly wait. Yes, it could change tonight. I know. It'll be fun, though. Maybe we can have it on the patio. Okay, take care." She hung up.

"Excuse me, was that about the Marcia Schallum book signing?"

"Yes, it was."

"It's tomorrow?"

"Late morning. Probably about eleven. Although the college is really wanting to host it. They're trying to move around events so that they can have space there. So, to be honest, we're not one-hundred percent sure."

"Can I give you my number—"

She laughed. "Presumptuous."

"Hardly."

The woman smiled and then blew her nose in a tissue.

Kilbraide took a step back. "I'd like to know where the signing will be. Can you let me know when it's confirmed?"

She slid a pad of paper and Kilbraide scribbled his number. "You, uh, from around here?"

"Out of town. Just visiting."

"That's interesting."

"What is?"

"You're the second man today who's stopped in and asked about her."

"Really?" Kilbraide was quiet.

"Yep. Another guy was here this morning asking."

"No kidding? Did he, uh, give a name?"

"No." The woman laughed once and then chuckled.

"What's funny?"

"Nothing, really. Except that it's weird to have two men like yourselves, you know, kind of stiff like military types." She smiled and Kilbraide could tell she wanted to say something.

"You're smiling again, what's up?" He coaxed her with his own smile.

"Not to sound racist or anything, but you're both black, too. It's all just quite rare in Saratoga." She smiled and playfully raised a fist. "BLM, you know?"

"I see."

CHAPTER NINETEEN

A mind has the ability to zip in a million directions at the snap of a finger. And that's what Kilbraide's was doing as he walked back from the Steak House where he had dinner in the outdoor dining area, trying not to notice the couples chatting with each other while eating.

Memories of his ex-wife crossed his mind. He missed that type of casual small-talk and he longed for the intimacy of a relationship, sharing your life with someone you trusted. But duty to his country always came first and his commitment to Lady Liberty interfered with the woman he had once loved.

What about Catalonia? He laughed at how stress played with the emotions. Something about her was very attractive, but how could he ever trust her?

He was still hungry after only having eaten a petite serving of filet mignon, sautéed asparagus, salad, and lots of water. A beer would have been great and so would a man-sized slab of meat, but he needed to be nimble and have his mind sharp. Catalonia had buzzed him and didn't see any evidence that Stevens was staying in a local motel.

Kilbraide figured as much. Stevens would either be up in a hide taking catnaps until dawn broke or sleeping out of town in some obscure location, but he liked to stay close to his target as though he was meditating on the prey. Kilbraide decided that he'd scope out the town, check out the neighborhood around the bookstore to see if he missed any clues, and head out to the college to scout it and see if he could detect Stevens' location.

The town's history made Kilbraide think about the natural limitations that colonial armies used to live with, like little to no fighting in winter and no attacks in formation in the dead of night. But the Revolutionary War era had cloak and dagger spies roaming the cities and countryside, eavesdropping up close which was remarkable. Imagine what those men would think of today's technology, along with two Black men playing a deadly game of cat and mouse.

Kilbraide reached the Bed and Breakfast, walked through the front door, made his way up the steps, and noticed a small package leaning against his door. He stepped cautiously and studied it for unusual markings or odd sounds. But there was nothing except a plain paper wrapping with his name on it. He touched the edge with his toe and stepped back. The package moved but nothing happened. He leaned down, picked it up, tore off the wrapping and had to catch his breath. It was a book and Marsha Schallum was the author. He opened it and—he tried to swallow but air caught in his throat as he read her inscription.

"*To Brian … life is short* …. What the hell?"

The enemy had never invaded his base during his tenure in the military. He always hunted them on their turf, but he never had to contend with them intruding on his personal space.

This was new territory.

Anger built and was turning to rage. Kilbraide calmed himself, placed the keycard against the door's sensor, turned the handle, and waited before stepping inside. The light was on as he had left it. He checked the bathroom and the closet where the gear looked untouched. The bed frame was solid against the floor so no intruder could wait under there. He tossed the book onto the bed and called Catalonia.

"Yeah, Kilbraide, what's up?" She sounded tired.

"Security's been breached. You guys getting sloppy or what?"

"What're you talking about?"

"I just got back from dinner and someone, I guess it was Stevens, left a lovely present in front of my door."

"What was it?"

"A copy of Marcia Schallum's book, that's what. And, yes, I'm okay. Thanks for asking."

"You're talking, so I assume you are. What about the book?"

"On the inside cover was a heartfelt inscription written to me."

"How about that? Maybe one day it'll be worth something," said Catalonia, with a hint of sarcasm. "What'd it say?"

Kilbraide thought he heard a smile in her voice. *So, what? She's joking now?* Kilbraide read the message to her.

"All right, we'll get on it," said Catalonia. "Your cover's blown so head back to the *bird* for the night."

"Yeah?"

"I'll alert the crew. Someone'll be standing by."

"I'm not heading back immediately. I have work to do. Leaving this gift for me is way out of character for him."

"Let me know when you're secure for the night."

"Yeah, I will."

He hung up and grabbed his rifle case in the closet. It was a good way to release adrenaline and get mentally prepared. He pressed his thumb against the fingerprint reader. It beeped and the case unlocked. He lifted the lid to reveal the latest weaponry: the Barret MRAD PSR, precision sniper rifle. He quickly assembled it and then disassembled it once and then twice.

The action was like a meditation mantra and it calmed him, a ritual of preparation. He was on a mission he didn't want, but he had a job to do. He placed the rifle back in its case, concealed it, and packed it, along with his belongings, securely in the car's trunk. Then he drove into the dark and made his way to the college.

The trip didn't take long in the small town and he parked just off campus. The lecture hall was close by. He studied the walkway from an adjacent parking lot and scanned the dozen or so trees that lined it. He walked quickly so he wouldn't look like he was loitering in the dark. There was a building to one side with a larger, more mature oak that had a network of branches.

Kilbraide made a circle around one building and then another, checking the rooftops. Not seeing signs of Stevens, he headed toward the still-open eateries just off campus. Alleyways glowed with the soft lights of the bars and were filled with the chatter of late-night diners. He headed to the sidewalk and looked up and down the street.

Then he made his way back to the car, committing the layout of the area to memory. There were many places for Stevens to set up unnoticed, but depending on where the event was staged, getting a clear shot at Schallum wouldn't be easy.

Kilbraide was thankful there was at least one thing in his favor. He pondered the irony that an internet legend at his global headquarters could feel invincible yet be quite vulnerable. A well-known senator could feel like he's in control of his own destiny and yet be taken down without warning. Strange how those were easier kills than bagging a pseudo-celebrity in a small town.

Where could Stevens be? How many quiet alleyways and secluded rooftops were there between the college and the bookstore?

He'd check it out. He got in his car and drove slowly away. He looked in his rear-view mirror out of habit and thought he saw a shadowy figure move quickly from behind a large tree trunk and toward the row of restaurant lights. Kilbraide slowed, turned right onto a street, and backtracked.

***

Stevens saw the car pull away. As he headed toward town, he spotted a lone bench on the edge of campus beneath a tree, and it looked too inviting to pass up. He needed a moment, pulled out his phone, and dialed Amanda, who he imagined by his side.

Her voice mail came on.

"Hey Amanda, just thinking about you and wanted to hear your voice. My business trip has been extended and I'll let you know when I'm on my way back. Hope you're well. See you soon."

Stevens wondered if Kilbraide had felt his presence on campus or picked up the vibration. They were kindred spirits after all, fighting for the same cause even if Kilbraide refused to acknowledge it. He looked toward town, got up, and started walking. Small college campuses had a way of spawning nightlife, no matter how tame.

He headed into a pub he had carefully surveyed earlier in the evening. It had a back exit that opened into an alleyway with a scene of its own, where local musicians played to intimate crowds on the back patio. Other pubs and restaurants added to the festive atmosphere with their own areas for dining and entertainment. It was easy to walk in the front door, out the back, and into another bar or coffee shop if necessary.

The intel was working better than Stevens expected so he took his phone, stood near the back door, and dialed.

"Yeah?" The answer was gruff.

"Are you reading the book?" asked Stevens.

Dead silence on the other end and, then Kilbraide chuckled. "Why am I not surprised that you have my number?"

"I'm a pro just like you. She's a nut case, isn't she?" Stevens teased. "I leafed through the pages. Total bullshit about how America is racist and corrupt. Don't get sucked into the hatred, Kilbraide."

There was quiet and then a reply. "And what about you? Are you sucked into the hatred?"

"I think Schallum's an idiot and she's dangerous to the America that I swore an oath to protect. I'm just following orders and doing my job. My cause is just."

"How so?"

"You know how so. You swore the same oath."

"Yes, I did," said Kilbraide. "To protect. Not to be the judge, jury, and executioner of innocent people."

"Just doing my job," said Stevens, "taking out people who are destroying our country."

"There are other ways."

"Other ways don't work. Their poison has seeped into every aspect of our culture. They're a brainwashed TikTok generation."

Kilbraide went with the flow. "You mean like the runny nose girl at the bookstore?"

"Yeah." Stevens was caught off-guard.

"I heard that I missed you there."

"Did she tell you that?"

"She did."

Stevens was matter-of-fact. "That makes sense. We're both on the same trail. I'm hunting a target and you're hunting me. The HOG and PIG. Hunter of gunmen and the professionally instructed gunman. Sooner or later, we're going to cross paths. We've actually done that now. I saw you scoping out the campus a while ago."

"Did you?"

"I did. Do you think that's where she's going to sign her wonderful books?"

"Maybe." Kilbraide was non-committal.

"Maybe the bookstore? Either place. I'm ready."

"Me, too."

"You going to stop me?"

"I am."

"Good luck with that. But since nothing is going to happen until tomorrow, why don't we act like gentlemen? Let's sit down and have a beer, face-to-face and brother-to-brother."

Stevens walked toward the parking lot. "I feel like telling you where I am. The more I think about it, the more I think we should sit down and have a beer, talk things over."

He felt in control since Kilbraide was a brother-in-arms. Plus, Vanguard had taken the bait and put Kilbraide on his trail like he had wanted. And this wasn't a game of cops and robbers because there'd be no arrest. This was life and death.

"You treating?" asked Kilbraide.

Stevens laughed. "Yeah, just like we're friendly rivals. Me, the big shot Marine who's treating you, the Army Ranger. We're both just trying to make the world a better place."

"What kind of beer do you like?"

"Any kind. As long as it foams beautifully in a frosty mug."

"Sounds good." Kilbraide sounded relaxed. "My throat's dry. Go ahead and buy us a couple."

"You serious?" The statement caught Stevens off guard.

"Yeah, go ahead. If you need me to pay you back, I will."

It sounded like Kilbraide was in a car that stopped, and his door opened.

Adrenaline was pumping through Stevens. It gave him a boost about a hundred times stronger than an energy drink. "Okay. What do you want me to get for you?"

"You choose," said Kilbraide. "Whatever you want. Some snooty, overpriced craft beer or a standard brand are both fine with me. Maybe we can become drinking buddies."

Stevens laughed. "Maybe. I doubt it. But I hope so."

Kilbraide could be walking along the sidewalk. There weren't that many bars to choose from. Maybe they could be friends and Kilbraide would rescue him, take him out of this desperate life and Stevens could tell him about Amanda.

"Okay, enough small talk. I'm going to buy us some beers," said Stevens, making his way into a pub.

"Great. I'm smacking my lips already."

Stevens got to the bar and motioned to the bartender.

"Yeah, just a minute," said the bartender, wiping his hands on a cloth.

Stevens covered the phone and his heart was pounding. What if Kilbraide suddenly appeared and stopped him from killing another person? The thought made Stevens feel light-hearted. Then his mind would be clear and he could sit down and write his own bestselling memoir.

"What's up?" asked the bartender, some young guy with scruffy blond hair pulled into a man bun who barely looked old enough to drink.

"Two of your finest craft beers," said Stevens.

"You got it, pal." The man stepped away.

Stevens spoke into the phone. "Okay, Kilbraide. The beer's ordered."

"Now all you have to do is tell me where you are."

Stevens smirked and was sweating at the thrill of the cat and mouse game. "Listen for a second."

He pulled the phone away from his ear and held it up to capture the noise. "Hear the music? You're a good detective. Figure it out. I'll see you soon." He clicked off the phone and spoke to the bartender who just delivered the beer. "The drinks are for Brian Kilbraide. He'll be here momentarily."

"Sure, boss."

Stevens thought about perching on a stool but changed his mind. He hurried out back, along the edge of the parking lot, and walked quickly through the darkness to his car.

CHAPTER TWENTY

A man in rimless glasses with an arm around a giggling woman weaved along the sidewalk, bumping once and then twice into Kilbraide as he tried to hurry past.

"Hey, chill, Dude," said the man.

The couple didn't make it far before stumbling into a dive bar.

Kilbraide poked his head in the doorway to see if the music inside matched what he had heard over his phone. It didn't. He hurried down the sidewalk and dialed, keeping his adrenaline in check and staying focused.

"Yeah, Kilbraide?" Catalonia spoke in her usual clipped voice.

"Guess who I got a call from?"

"Yeah, we heard."

"Did you get a trace?"

"No trace available. Signal's a global hop. Says the call originated in the Philippines. Voice was scrambled on this end. What do you got?"

"He's here. I'm on his trail heading inside a bar."

"I'll get a team on the way."

"No, not yet," said Kilbraide, taking a breath. "Let me get back to you."

"I'll be standing by. How're you holding up?"

Kilbraide was surprised. "Just peachy. Thanks for asking."

"Don't let it go to your head."

The phone clicked dead.

That was a nice touch. Kilbraide felt a bit of a lift as he hurried from one pub to another, listening to hear if the music and chatter was similar to the background noise on the surprise call. He found one and tried to push inside, but a man with lots of beer on his breath was standing in the doorway and slurring his words as he chatted with a coed who had a little too much to drink and was wobbling on her heels.

"You're creating a fire hazard, aren't you?" asked Kilbraide, lowering his shoulder, turning, and squeezing by.

The man mumbled something unintelligible as Kilbraide headed inside listening to casual chatter, peals of laughter, and the clatter of glasses and mugs behind the bar.

He scanned the dimly lit room trying to pick out Stevens. One man who was in the corner resembled him, but he was playing chess with a friend. Another man stood near the front, cozying up with some woman. Several people sat on barstools with their backs to him, slouching forward.

Stevens was always ramrod straight.

"Hey, over here."

Kilbraide glanced instinctively, but it was nothing, except someone shouting near the restroom. The back door had a lit *Exit* sign. He made his way, stepped out into the alley, and looked at the tables from the other eateries. Stevens was nowhere to be seen.

Kilbraide quickly checked the parking lot and the street. Nothing.

The adrenaline finished its run and left him feeling deflated.

He stepped back into the bar and motioned for the bartender. "Hey, have you seen a guy in here not too long ago? Ordered a couple of beers."

The bartender looked at him. "Just about everybody here orders beer. Look around."

"He was a Black guy, kind of stiff, prim and proper."

"Yeah," said the bartender, pointing to two mugs. "He ordered the best—our House Special. Brewed locally and available nationally. It's for people who crave a premium taste. That'll be twenty-five dollars."

Kilbraide looked at the foamy mugs. *Son-of-a-bitch.*

CHAPTER TWENTY-ONE

Kilbraide made his way back to the jet and met one of the armed crew members who let him in for a few hours of rest. Inside the fuselage, there was a hive of activity with people monitoring computer screens and typing away.

"Wow, are you guys all work and no play—and no sleep?" asked Kilbraide.

"Just enough corruption in this world to keep all of us busy," replied one of the surveillance technicians.

"Where do I get some rest?"

The man pointed to a doorway separating everyone from the back of the cabin. Kilbraide opened the door to see a sofa made into a bed. He set his gear down and stretched out. He visualized the town's layout as he closed his eyes and imagined how and where Stevens would lie in wait. It seemed like an impossible task because of the way Stevens normally operated.

How the hell would he get Schallum in his sights, unless he had something like a pistol and would take her out in close range? No. Too risky for him. He didn't want to get caught. He wasn't going to be John Wilkes Booth closing in on President Lincoln. But—who knows, could it ever be an option?

Stevens would plan on having distance.

The phone call from Stevens shook Kilbraide, but only for a moment. How the hell did he know his whereabouts? *Black Eagle's got damned good intel.* And the beer was too bitter. Not worth the twenty bucks.

He texted Catalonia to tell her that he was secure for the night.

***

Kilbraide thought through the previous day as he woke. For some reason, Stevens really wanted his attention. He rolled his legs off the narrow bed, sat up, and quickly assembled and disassembled his rifle. He did it once and then a second time. The action felt good and prepared him for whatever would happen.

The funny thing was Kilbraide wasn't worried about his own life. He knew Stevens would never fire a shot at him unless he was completely desperate and caught in a corner. But even then, Stevens was on a strange mission, and he wanted company on the journey.

The sun was up, and it was time to go. He grabbed his phone and read a text message from the bookstore. The signing was definitely scheduled for the college.

Damn. Stevens was quite a pro and a warrior, thought Kilbraide as he scrolled through his phone for the day's headlines and the weather. Mostly clear skies with patchy white clouds. Beautiful day for an assassination.

He pocketed his phone, grabbed his gear, and lugged it to the front. A plate of eggs, sausage, and toast was waiting.

"Compliments of the boss," said a technician he hadn't met before.

How did the personnel come and go so quickly? Kilbraide wondered. He ate breakfast and right before he stepped out one of the techs gave him news.

"Highs in the low 70s today—"

"Yeah, and winds coming in from the northeast at up to 10 miles per hour. Thanks," said Kilbraide, opening the door and stepping outside.

***

Stevens woke in the bare-bones motel room with furniture made from thinly, pressed particle board. He stretched and checked his phone. A text from the bookstore confirmed that the signing was scheduled for the college. Martha Schallum wanted to address the students when she was done.

She won't get a chance, mused Stevens.

The weather looked favorable, and he'd adjust his aim for any breezes.

He grabbed a bagel from a grocery bag he picked up the night before, munched it, and settled into his preparation by assembling and disassembling his rifle.

Stevens had just enough sleep to feel strong. He slipped into maintenance coveralls, packed his belongings, and decided it was time to go. He felt good about choosing the roof of the pub where he ordered the beers and using it as his hide.

Would Kilbraide pick up on the hint of where he'd be?

He drove near the edge of restaurant row, parked, and grabbed the duffle bag with his necessary gear. The rifle was disassembled inside and wrapped in its own thick vinyl case.

He had decided on the pub since she had chosen the college. Not only because it was strategically located and the roof had a parapet to hide his movements, but also because it was too obvious as the perfect choice. Hide in plain sight. Kilbraide would never guess.

Getting to the roof wasn't even a challenge. It was almost too easy. In the back alley was a maintenance ladder attached to the rear of the pub. Numerous shade trees that wouldn't pass the fire code hid most of the ladder from view. It was a piece of cake.

Stevens didn't hesitate as he grabbed the first rung, strung his bag on his back, and started the climb up. His hand slipped once, but he recovered and made his way to the roof, looking like any heating and air conditioning maintenance man.

He was getting settled when a faint buzzing sound caught his attention. A drone was heading toward him. He grabbed the duffel bag, slid beneath metal ductwork, and waited several seconds. The buzzing grew fainter, and all was clear. Time to set up.

***

Kilbraide piloted the drone back to his position and had it land at his feet. Stevens had to be nearby. He set the drone to *autonomous* and it flew off with a high-pitched buzz. While making his way to the Quad, Kilbraide used his phone to monitor the drone's progress. Students with backpacks walked between buildings and Kilbraide motioned to a security guard. "Any word on what time the book signing will be?"

The guard nodded, looked at his watch, and pointed to a few maintenance workers setting up rope barriers along the sidewalk. "Soon. That's the best I can tell you. I don't know what's going on. It was supposed to be out here near the walkway, but they moved it inside."

"Oh, yeah?" Kilbraide glanced around the front of the building.

"Yeah. Like heightened security or something. Hell, this is just a small college. This isn't like the campus of ProfileScene. Man, they still haven't found the son-of-a-bitch who did that."

"I'm sure they're working on it." Kilbraide smiled, glad he had earlier called in a threat to the tip line. One more obstacle for Stevens to overcome.

The guard reached in his pocket, pulled out a key ring, and swung it around his finger. "Yeah, it's going to be in the auditorium. Invite only for folks in town."

"That sucks."

"Do you teach here?"

"No. I'm just a fan of hers and was hoping to a glimpse up close."

"Too bad. All faculty and students are welcome."

Kilbraide shrugged.

The guard scrunched his face. "Big fan, huh? I'll tell you what. Reporters will be here, too. Lots of wine and cheese on hand." He smiled. "Of course, invite only is BS for the press. Bring a pen and notebook and I'll get you in if you want. You like wine and cheese?"

"Yeah."

"They're going to have lots of it. Come back in a while and we'll see what we can do."

"Sure, thanks. That'd be great," said Kilbraide. "I might just take you up on it."

"Sounds good, boss. In the meantime, I'm grabbing me a coffee."

"Thanks for the info." Kilbraide walked across the quad with his eye on a grove of trees in the distance? Could Stevens be in their shadows? Time to check the drone.

He sat on a bench under a shade tree, and using his phone's screen, took control of the drone. He flew it across the street to the line of businesses, surveying their roofs. There were plenty of heating and air conditioning units giving good cover to take a shot. But it was too obvious, too easy. Stevens liked a challenge.

Kilbraide flew the drone over the next building and noticed it was the pub where Stevens *didn't* buy him a drink. For a second, he felt like Stevens had purposely led him to the spot.

No, it couldn't be that obvious.

***

Stevens used his laser rangefinder to measure distances to the sidewalk and determine the angle. He pulled out his wind gauge when that familiar high pitch buzzing sound alerted him. The drone. He caught a glimpse and ducked again beneath the ductwork with his face hitting and scraping against the roof. He gently tugged his bag close to shield him from view.

***

Kilbraide made one pass and then another with the drone over the top of the building and saw no movement, nothing unusual. Not even a way to get on the roof unless you climbed one of the shade trees. Kilbraide moved on to get a close look at each building down the row.

As he came up empty, his insides were uneasy. *Where the hell was Stevens?*

CHAPTER TWENTY-TWO

Stevens had used his rangefinder to scan the nearby roofs for any sign of Kilbraide. Nowhere in sight. Then he noted how the temperature rose and the breeze grew still. He had become an expert in the slightest of atmospheric changes and adjusted accordingly. The threat of the drone flying low and possibly locking in on him had unnerved him, so he stayed crouched with his muscles tense between his hiding place beneath the ductwork and his vantage point behind the parapet.

Minutes teased him as they ticked as slowly as possible, and he struggled to find that internal rhythm that allowed him to focus. He drew on his experience, grabbed his rifle, and quickly assembled it. Then he disassembled it before putting it back together. The repetition was working.

Amanda.

Not now.

Poison was spreading rapidly in everyone's minds: the erosion of American values, the decline into socialism and then communism. He would have nothing to live for if he didn't stop the evil. To hell with the drone.

Disassemble the weapon—and then assemble. Disassemble. Assemble. The rhythm was building.

And that's when he heard the light squeal of brakes. He rolled from beneath the ductwork, crouched behind the parapet, and studied the activity below. There were two cars pulling up and a group of people moving along the rope barriers toward the street. Security guards stood on both sides of the sidewalk.

They unwittingly created an opening and Stevens got in position, lying prone with the barrel of his rifle aimed through an opening in the parapet. He had a clear line of sight at the sidewalk. He looked through the riflescope, a perfect view. Stevens slid the bolt back and chambered the round. The guards were doing a great job at keeping people away. And then the doors of the cars opened. Marcia Schallum and her entourage emerged in full view.

Adrenaline pumped through his body. Stevens rested the pad of his index finger on the trigger and took a deep breath to calm himself. His target took one step forward and—two laughing young ladies waved and ducked beneath the rope barrier with a bouquet of flowers.

Wait for it.

Stevens slid his finger off the trigger.

Schallum took the flowers and seemed like she was settling in for a friendly chat when Security intervened and escorted the fans back behind the rope. One of the people who had gotten out of the car with her moved in behind, an attractive woman who patted her shoulder, smiled and ushered Schallum toward the entrance of the auditorium.

This was it, the *apricot.* The perfect shot where the top of the spine and the brain meet, and a bullet topples the victim without reflex.

Wait.

Another member of her entourage walked right behind Schallum, shielding the back of her head from Stevens' view.

Too many fans. Not a clean shot. Collateral damage would sink the mission.

There was plenty of time since the walkway was long, like the entrance to a stately cathedral. The woman who had patted Schallum's shoulder moved on, but then the security guards began undoing the rope barrier and the crowd started moving up the sidewalk.

Stevens kept breathing, slowing the rhythm of his heart, tracking her through his scope and waiting for the right moment when her head centered in his crosshairs.

Patience.

Then suddenly and for some strange reason the crowd parted and Schallum was completely vulnerable as she neared the entrance to the auditorium. Stevens started pressing the trigger and opened his mouth to relax and equalize the pressure in his inner ear from the blast of the gunshot. Amanda intruded on his thoughts as Schallum stepped inside, disappearing from view as a crowd closed in behind her.

Stevens was sweating. He hesitated and didn't take the shot. He would wait.

***

Kilbraide was caught off guard when Schallum arrived. She was earlier than what security had said and he didn't have time to make it to his own vantage point, the top of the roof of the auditorium. Meanwhile, the drone hadn't relayed any suspicious movements on the tops of the buildings, in the surrounding trees, or along the sidewalk. But when Schallum made it inside unharmed, he was thankful but puzzled.

He landed the drone, packed it up, and headed up a back stairway to the roof of the auditorium. He took a position near a vent, assembled his rifle, and looked out over the campus. In the building below him, Schallum was busily signing books and chatting, either not caring that she was a target or somehow feeling invincible.

The threat of an assassination inside was almost nil.

Kilbraide imagined the scene. A local reporter holding a notepad, talking to her, while trying to write, sip wine, and munch cheese at the same time. Adoring fans waiting for autographs.

He wondered how many *reporters* the security guard had let in.

Maybe Stevens was down there. Not his operating style even though he had spoken to her in the studio.

Then he turned his attention to the town where he looked through his riflescope and scanned the buildings. Sun glistened off the windows of passing cars and he had to squint in the glare. Trying to find Stevens from this vantage point was next to impossible. So he took the drone, set it on autopilot, and sent it into flight again.

An hour went by quickly and it wasn't long before he heard commotion in the quad. People were chatting away and waving goodbye to Marcia Schallum who was exiting out the front.

Damn.

Kilbraide was surprised. He looked closely at his phone's screen monitoring the drone's camera and didn't see anything at first, but then he noticed a slight movement on the roof of the pub. *Shit.*

Stevens—in position.

Schallum was on the sidewalk.

***

The discipline of a warrior paid off.

But at the very moment Stevens caught Schallum alone and in his sights a wild buzzing kicked in and suddenly he was smacked in the face. The propellers cut like razors and knocked him sideways from both force and total surprise. He nearly fired but pulled his finger away.

The drone was on the roof, spinning in a circle, disabled from the impact. Stevens pounced on the faceless intruder.

He looked across the quad and saw his target getting into the back seat of a car as it pulled away.

"Good work, Kilbraide." He smiled, gave a thumbs up into the camera, and then smashed the drone with his foot. His adrenaline was pumping as hard as if he had fired the rifle. He disassembled the weapon within seconds. He then packed up everything, ran across the roof toward the alley, climbed down the ladder and got the hell out of sight.

***

The last thing Kilbraide saw was Steven's face before his phone's screen went blank. His detective instincts kicked in. He tossed his equipment bag over the rifle then ducked in the rooftop doorway and sped down the stairs. An older man with glasses, holding a cup of coffee, was walking up, nearly in the middle of the stairwell and got elbowed against the wall.

"Hey," came the shout.

But Kilbraide was out the back door, racing across the quad, and heading toward the pub. He ran behind the building to the alley and saw a car squeal out of the parking lot. He pulled his pistol as a horn blared. He spun to find that he was blocking the driveway and another driver was trying to exit the lot. The driver saw the gun and raised her hands. Kilbraide turned back to the first car. It was gone.

He holstered his gun. The female driver flipped him off and yelled some profanity about abolishing the Second Amendment as she drove down the alley.

Kilbraide shook his head. He missed Stevens, but at least Marcia Schallum was still alive.

CHAPTER TWENTY-THREE

Kilbraide climbed the ladder to the rooftop of the pub and studied the surrounding area. Had he made a huge mistake in his own judgment? Did he depend too heavily on the drone surveillance instead of relying on his riflescope?

He picked up the broken drone and steadied his nerves, then took out his phone and called Catalonia.

"Yeah? What's the news?"

Kilbraide laid it out. "I stopped Stevens."

"You killed him?"

"I made him miss his chance." Kilbraide was catching his breath.

Catalonia was tense. "What do you mean?"

"He was on a rooftop, and I flew the drone into his head. Hit him real hard."

"What? Where is he now?"

"He took off." Kilbraide was furious at Catalonia for putting him in such an awful situation.

"I want him dead."

"I couldn't get a shot off."

"So he's gone?"

"Well, he's not where he was."

Silence.

Kilbraide tried again. "Look, I just saved someone's life."

"Your assignment was to take someone's life. That's what you're known for."

The whole thing was crazy. Catalonia. The techies on the jet. Black Ops fighting Black Ops—like some kind of demented chess game. *What the hell am I doing here?*

"What I'm known for is kills on the battlefield, taking out enemy combatants," Kilbraide protested. "This is some little tourist town with a small college. It's a different world."

"You're on a mission, Kilbraide. You have your orders. Follow them."

"The guy's lying on the roof of a pub, hidden behind a wall. Camouflaged. And I'm on top of a campus auditorium. It's not that easy." His anger boiled over. "I'm a detective, for Christ's sake."

"You're a sniper who let your target get away."

Kilbraide settled and tried to determine his next moves.

"Could you have taken a shot?" asked Catalonia.

"That's not the damn question to ask—"

"Why didn't you take the shot?"

"I was caught off guard. I had one eye on Schallum, another on the drone. I didn't have time."

Catalonia didn't respond.

"I saved her life for God's sake," said Kilbraide. "Doesn't that mean anything?"

"In most circumstances, yes."

Kilbraide imagined a chess board and Catalonia coldly knocking out the opposing pieces as she continued.

"All I care about is Stevens and he's still breathing."

"Look, he's with Black Eagle and you're running Vanguard. I'm feeling like this is a pissing competition. Do the smart thing. If you're so worried about Stevens disrupting whatever it is that you're trying to accomplish—and I wonder what the hell that is exactly … look, you want him stopped? Then go to whoever's in charge. Put a terminate order on Black Eagle."

"Easier said than done. They're incredibly decentralized and the hierarchy changes continuously. Hell, they don't even know who they are."

"Okay, then. Just go to the president. You know, the guy in the White House. Tell him to put a stop to it."

"Wishful thinking," said Catalonia, "but it doesn't work that way."

"What do you mean?"

"The president's not in the know."

"What?"

"He's only a temporary employee. Like you. But different. He doesn't know and he has no need to know the inner workings of what actually keeps this country running."

Suddenly, Kilbraide felt sick. What the hell happened to America? Some shadow government was ordering him to fight some other part of the shadow government. *Am I that naïve? Is this the way it really works?*

He thought that working for LAPD would clue him in on just about everything. That he'd be powerful to stop crime as a detective. Now he felt like a no-one. And his own head could explode into red mist if he didn't toe the line.

"You there, Kilbraide?" Catalonia's voice shook him.

"Unfortunately, yes."

"The orders are clear. Eliminate Stevens. It's that simple."

"Yeah, eazy-peazy as shit. All I have to do is figure out where he went and what Schallum's doing."

"She's booked on a flight tomorrow morning, no further engagements here. At the moment, she's on her way to lunch with her entourage, but we're not sure exactly where or what she's doing after that."

"You sure know a lot, don't you?" Kilbraide was more disgusted than impressed.

"It's our job. And I suggest you get off your ass and do yours."

The line went dead. Catalonia terminated the call without saying goodbye.

All business—and a heart of ice.

CHAPTER TWENTY-FOUR

Marcia Schallum repelled fear like titanium repelled burning temperatures and gun shots. She was invincible in her own mind. Not that she was careless, even though she was outspoken in her beliefs, but she considered herself courageous. She never listened to opposing views, only giving their opinions lip service while she impatiently waited for the chance to interrupt their views with her own righteous beliefs. And for that, Marcia had an eclectic fanbase that hung on her every word like gospel.

She felt even more secure sitting in an upholstered chair in the bedroom where she grew up. She stared out the bedroom window into the night and contemplated her successful career. Her mother was resting quietly downstairs. It was here where Marcia had typed book reports and edited articles for the student newspaper. Home was a fortress.

Across the room, on the edge of the bed, her assistant, Jeanine Gravilos, loosened the button of her blouse. And then the next button. She smiled at Marcia, kicked off her heels and fell back on the mattress.

"I never expected to go on a wild adventure in Saratoga. Damn, this city is a bore. Unless you like horse racing, but that should be banned, so cruel. Hey, I have an idea for excitement." Jeanine propped herself on her elbows and invitingly opened her legs.

"The city has had a lifetime of characters, colorful history, and it's a quiet place to raise a family," said Schallum, getting up, crossing the room, and plopping down on the mattress alongside Jeanine.

"You sound like a Republican."

Schallum acted wounded and playfully slapped her companion. "I wasn't finished. I was about to say it's a good place to raise a family, especially since we're plenty Blue up here. City council, schoolboards—"

"Whew. You scared me there for a minute."

"But you're right. This town is a bore and I'm ready to get back to Manhattan. The signings are fun, but it's the same stupid small talk with people I've met a dozen times."

Jeanine was a much-needed balm. The relationship was kept from the public, mostly because Marcia loved the intimate moments with her, like hugging a comfy pillow that never goes out of style. She didn't need to share that with anybody.

"You did well today." Jeanine complimented her boss, turning her head to kiss her gently.

"I know. And you're going to reward me how?" said Schallum, smiling, and running a teasing finger along Jeanine's lips.

***

Stevens was brimming with quiet confidence as he watched the bedroom that was still well lit. He had a clear view of the women seducing each other. This was a perfect hide. He was ready, perched on a dark rooftop bordering the commercial and residential sections. Only 300 yards away. An easy kill.

Schallum stood, undid her designer jeans but then stepped across the room and out of the fine lines of the reticle, the crosshairs.

Wait.

She returned in her bra and panties, stretching across the bed, nuzzling and undressing her assistant.

Wait.

***

Kilbraide walked quickly in an alleyway behind Schallum's place when a scuffling startled him. He held his breath, drew his handgun, turned, and watched a raccoon scurry away from a backyard.

He exhaled. "Damn creatures."

Kilbraide's heart was pounding and he was out of breath after searching for a workable location. Older homes with peaked roofs mixed with one-story office buildings didn't do the job. But now, he located a rundown building once used as a hotel that was now vacant and under renovation. He made his way inside to a second-story window, scanning the neighborhood with an infrared riflescope attachment.

Schallum's house was close, but he couldn't find Stevens, an expert at blending with the surrounding environment.

***

Schallum lay on her back with her head resting on a feather pillow.

Jeanine's eyes were filled with love and anticipation. Her fingers were gentle, tracing Schallum's nose, lips, and chin. Her kisses were delicate—one on the forehead, the other on the cheek, and the last one on her lips. Deliberate. Gentle. Kind.

Schallum closed her eyes and soaked in the pleasurable vibrations of her assistant's touch.

***

Stevens breathed and let the world fade completely so he had only one scene to focus on. No distractions. This was it. This was his life. This was his mission. He was careful. Calculated. *One shot. One kill.* He was that good. No collateral damage, ever. The signal sent was clearer that way—pointing out who the enemy was and the danger that was being wrought on the whole country.

Let the kissing continue. Let the lovemaking be. Stevens knew that every split second that ticked away was bringing the target closer to its fate. He peered through the scope, absorbing the moment with his finger poised on the trigger.

Breathe.

Wait.

Breathe.

Wait.

Timing was everything. The moment had to be right. One Kill Shot. No collateral damage he repeated to himself over and over like a mantra as he stood ready.

The passion between the two women intensified. The assistant kissed her way down Schallum's stomach.

Breathe.

Wait.

Now.

The moment arrived. The women lost control in their passions. Schallum arched her back and then quickly sat up as a cry of ecstasy escaped her lips. Stevens pressed the trigger and sent the round shattering the window, and exploding out the back of Marcia Schallum's head.

A perfect shot.

The tedious hours spent plotting and waiting were now rewarded and Stevens quickly, methodically packed his weapon as simply as packing a bag for an overnight trip. He pulled out his calling card, the patch that read *One Shot, One Kill*, grabbed a pen from his pocket, and started to scribble but stopped. No need to write Kilbraide's name on this one.

He's on the hunt.

He positioned it so it could easily be found by the authorities.

He needed no thanks. No congratulations. The hit was scored, and the country was now a safer place. Within seconds, he was on his way down from the hide, slipping into the darkness to his car. Before driving away, he sent a one-word text: *Done.*

***

Kilbraide heard the familiar report of a suppressed round, instantly followed by breaking glass. He knew he had failed when a moment later the cries of anguished screaming pierced the quiet night.

CHAPTER TWENTY-FIVE

The only thing worse than being eaten alive by lions, thought Kilbraide, is waiting to be eaten alive. A windowless conference room with drab walls was the perfect place to have that feeling. He sat on a vinyl chair that seemed chilly, or maybe it was his nerves. Minutes passed and while Kilbraide sat alone he decided he'd stay calm and not think through any defense. He wasn't a school kid sitting in the principal's office. Let Catalonia speak. See what direction she goes in.

His solitary torture ended when Catalonia entered the room holding a cup of coffee and a laptop. No questions like "How are you?" and no way in hell was there a "Good to see you."

She sipped her coffee with one hand and powered up her laptop with the other. Monitors on the wall lit up, showing news outlets with similar disturbing headlines. The *Washington Post* simply proclaimed: "Devastating."

Marcia Schallum's death was front page news above the fold while a headline farther down mentioned, "Still Nothing." The report's tone scolded local police and the FBI for no leads in the deaths of Julius Brae, Senator Alanasian, and now Marcia Schallum.

"You ought to see what the *New York Times* says." Catalonia's tone was like a sheet of ice covering a highway.

There was no way to respond to her comment. Some people had a natural ability to unnerve others by saying the bare minimum, and Catalonia was an expert.

"Or did you read it already?" she asked.

"No."

"You need to understand how serious this really is."

She set her coffee on the table and punched up a *LA Times* story that mentioned how people who knew Schallum were outraged and threatening violence. They'd find her counterparts with opposing views and hunt them down.

Catalonia's behavior and attitude angered Kilbraide. He could guess public reaction and didn't need news coverage to either affirm his work or send him on a guilt trip.

"I know how serious this is," said Kilbraide.

"Really? Then why'd you fuck up so badly?"

"It all falls on me? You work with such a big, hi-tech agency but you tossed me into this mess." Kilbraide wanted to pound his fist on the table. "I was a sniper in the military, in another country. And now I'm a cop. I'm not a hired assassin who hunts and kills Americans on American soil."

"As a police detective, you protect people by tracking down bad guys. That's what you were told to do here."

"Yes, I track down bad guys, and arrest them. But I also give them due process, not take them out at a thousand yards."

"You were a lot closer than that to Stevens."

"Hey, I've got a suggestion," said Kilbraide.

"What?"

"Use the proper channels of government to take him out. Like some congressional committee on intelligence matters."

"We've been over that. Too messy. Too many decision-makers involved and too many politicians who have no clue about what's going on. They only care about protecting their own asses and their pet projects." Catalonia aimed her gaze at Kilbraide. "I thought I had found my man."

"You have no idea, what it was like on the roof, looking at the students strolling by. Saratoga's a college town. A tourist area where some of the worst crimes are cars running stop signs.'"

Catalonia clenched her jaw. "Grow a pair, Kilbraide. You were in the Rangers for Christ's sake. We're going to have a full-fledged civil war between the left and the right if we don't stop Stevens. Stuff your sentimental feelings back into your ass where they belong and go kill the motherfucker. Is that clear?"

"Crystal," he muttered.

There was a lot to do like research Stevens' next potential targets. There were dozens of high-profile possibilities. He went for tech, an elected U.S. senator, then a media-driven personality, and all had far-reaching leftist views. Who's next? Who could really know? There was academia, big business. How could he narrow it down?

Kilbraide wasn't in a talking mood, especially if Catalonia was going to grind him down verbally. She looked busy, pounding the keypad on the computer, and assaulting the screen with her eyes. She was pissed.

"I almost forgot." She opened a briefcase that was on the conference table and pulled out a plastic evidence bag. "Our investigators found this at the site."

Stevens' trademark patch, *One Shot, One Kill*, was staring at Kilbraide.

"Strangely, your name's not on it this time," remarked Catalonia.

He wanted to punch a hole in the wall and needed to step out before he actually did.

"Excuse me. I think it's best if I go for a walk."

Kilbraide didn't wait for approval. He got up and left.

***

Kilbraide jogged around the perimeter of the complex. Groves of trees shielded him from the building so he could pretend he was alone, but he needed to get off the property. The Rockies were just to the west. He'd demand to go there for a day to think and soak up nature. Maybe that was an ingredient for Stevens' success. He wasn't stuck in conference rooms with the pressures of the world bearing down on him. He was an independent operator. He couldn't imagine Stevens sitting in a stupid boardroom with Black Eagle higher-ups.

Hiking in the Rockies was a must. He'd plead insanity if he had too. Although he'd be in good company. It seemed like Catalonia and everyone else were already insane.

Kilbraide slowed to a walk and breathed deeply. It was unlikely for Stevens to strike immediately after making a kill. There had to be time.

CHAPTER TWENTY-SIX

Stevens drove to his cabin, parked, and unloaded a case of beer and groceries from the back of his truck. A piece of white paper was on his door: *Saw you get in your truck this morning and wondered if you'd like to go out to watch a game and have a drink. PS, glad you're back.*

Amanda signed her name with *Bigg Huggz* and a little smiley face she had used when flirting with him in texts. It gave him a nice feeling that she seemed to be genuinely interested, but he was conflicted. Doubts told him he could never be with her, but he wondered why he invested so much time in her emotionally.

Don't get involved, don't get distracted.

She must have been keeping an eye out for his return.

He pulled the paper off the door, carried the beer and groceries inside, and decided it best to cut off communication before more of a relationship developed. Too much risk involved. Maybe it was time to move again. He didn't want to hurt her, but the thought of having a drink with her was appealing. It'd be relaxing and with good company. He started to call her, had second thoughts, and sent her a text: *Saw your note. Sounds great. What time?*

Doubt flooded his mind and there was no escaping the *What If?*

What if she was collaborating in some form, some capacity with who knows who or what? If it was law enforcement, then that would cause problems. Thinking about her was the easy part while being with her was the unknown.

Who is she? How did she know I was back? Is she just watching me and keeping tabs, stalking me, or does she really see something in me? Or in us? Like, a future?

Those questions never surfaced in his mind until now. At a distance, he could fantasize about her without anything at stake. But he really wanted to be with her. The options were antagonizing. If he told her that he wasn't available, then she could write him off and that would be the end. Or, he could say he got called out of town and not go out for drinks.

The positives of her smile and easy demeanor were outweighing the doubts.

Stevens felt like an electric current jolted him and he ignored his own concerns. He re-read the text he sent, sent her a blushing smiley face on impulse, and immediately regretted it, feeling as awkward as his first date in high school.

Maybe it was a mistake getting involved with her, but it was something he needed to do. A change. To feel normal again.

***

Kilbraide welcomed the ache in his legs as he wound up the path to the summit. No way would they keep him from running the trails. Fresh air. The Rockies. A chance to push himself. He'd be back soon enough but for now the peaks along the range were an impressive natural divide, separating the United States into east and west.

What it would be like to lose yourself in the wilderness?

His mind wandered as he took in the view of the permanent snowfields while the sun warmed him. He thought of his dad, a Vietnam Vet who said he was proud to serve his country despite the unrest of the civil rights movement and an unpopular war.

Kilbraide needed this moment to catch his breath, reflect, and realize what was good. Being out here was his favorite type of wild.

***

Lively chords from the band and the singer's twang made the country bar a comfortable place. Stevens liked all genres of music from urban to country, and even classical. The variety simply gave people of all backgrounds a chance to use their talents.

A TV with the sound turned down carried the Giants—Dodgers game.

Fortunately, the game was broadcast regionally so it wasn't likely to have news updates. The wall-to-wall coverage of ProfileScene had slowed down and the site had been back online for a while now. The

Media was sticking to the reports they first aired that it was Russian and North Korean hackers that took it down through a DOS attack.

The news media—nothing but propaganda and always looking for a boost in ratings, thought Stevens.

Coverage of Martha Schallum continued ad nauseam on the expected outlets, even though Stevens didn't think she was worth even one twenty-four-hour news cycle.

None of that mattered now, especially since a platter of freshly crisped nachos topped with ground beef, cheese, and salsa was ready for munching.

Stevens took a chip, crunched it, and swallowed, glad the propeller cut on his face was healing.

"Wait." Amanda's eyes were magnetic, and Stevens was glad she lifted her mug of beer that briefly hid her gaze. "Cheers." Her smile and voice warmed him more than a fire in a stone hearth.

"And cheers to you. Thank you for the invite. This is nice." He sipped his beer.

"You're quite welcome." She scrunched her face. "Hey, what happened?" She looked near his jaw.

"Dull razor. Cut myself shaving."

"You need to be more careful."

"Noted." Stevens started taking another bite.

"Before you ruin the dish." Amanda took another sip, set her mug on the table, pulled out her phone, and snapped a picture of the food.

She quickly took a selfie with the band in the background and before Stevens could object, she leaned over and captured an image of them.

"Now, you can eat up," she said.

The moment was dangerous but exhilarating, thought Stevens. He took another chip and wondered if, and where, she'd post it. He didn't like, nor want his picture posted anywhere. But what was he supposed to do? Grab the phone out of her hand? Delete her photo history? Yeah, maybe he would do that later when he had the chance. In the meantime, he wasn't going to worry about it, too much. The lighting was dim so recognition could be tough.

Stevens wondered. *What if Kilbraide saw it?*

"Thinking about something?" asked Amanda.

"Oh, nothing." Stevens forced a smile. "I always said that I'd never take selfies."

"You didn't." She laughed. "I took it for you."

He was relieved when she changed the subject.

"Oh, I meant to tell you that I walked by your place a few times. You know, just to make sure everything was okay."

He smiled. "Has everything been fine?"

"You had some unwanted visitors."

"Oh?" Stevens' stomach turned knots.

Amanda laughed. "Squirrels. They bombarded it with nuts."

"I can handle a few nuts." He relaxed.

"Hey, wait a minute. You're not implying that about me, are you?" she laughed.

"No, no. I didn't mean it like that."

Amanda glanced from Stevens to the band. "I know. I was just playing with you." She looked back to Stevens. "How was your trip? You sure had to leave quickly."

He gripped the mug. "Yeah. I, uh, am at the whims of people more powerful than me."

"Yeah. Aren't we all? Do tell." Amanda sounded intrigued.

"Financial management for individuals with a high net worth." He was repeating a well-rehearsed line.

"Fascinating." She smiled and took a drink.

"Yeah, boring stuff. Thinking of retirement, 'cause I'm not sure how much longer I can do this. But you're not interested."

"No, I am."

"Actually, as I just said, it's really boring stuff," said Stevens. "But on the other hand, it does have advantages and perks."

"Like lots of travel? Flying first class?"

"Yep. The only way to fly."

"So did you graduate from one of those fancy business schools like Wharton or, hmm, how about Stanford?"

"You ask a lot of questions," he smiled. "Nothing like that. Real humble. University of Virginia."

"Humble?" Amanda laughed. "You call UVA humble?"

"Where'd you graduate from?"

"Duke."

Stevens smiled. "Then UVA is humble."

"They're both similar. Rich traditions and rich families," said Amanda.

"So, do you like working for a big tech company?"

"Yeah. It's okay. I dream of traveling, backpacking someplace quiet. You know, getting away from it all?"

"Same here. Oh, bad memory. I forgot. Who do you work for again?"

"Zudder.com."

"Can't say I've been on that site. Of course, I don't spend time on social media."

Amanda agreed. "I understand. It has good and bad points."

"Yeah, addictive, biased, brainwashing," he laughed. "Maybe I'm just too old to understand it. Why do people want to put their lives on the internet for everyone to see and judge? Like with the selfie thing. Definitely not for me. Not sure my clients would want to see my face."

"Then they're missing out." She let her gaze linger.

"I'll take the compliment." Stevens sipped his beer. "So, what do you do at Zudder?"

"Develop software and handle issues related to licensing and intellectual property. Now, that's boring stuff." Her voice softened. "I still can't get over what happened at ProfileScene. I know a lot of people over there. So sad. It's devastating to think one of the most influential people in the world could be killed just like that." Amanda snapped her fingers. "And they still haven't found the idiot who did it. Crazy."

"I know."

"News and social media are saying it's all because of freedom of speech, censorship, and…I just can't believe that someone killed him over a difference of opinion. Then they killed that senator, and now Marcia Schallum. I mean, what's happening to our world?"

"I know. It's become a sad place. So, let's not talk current events." Stevens changed the subject. "We're here for a nice evening. Let's talk about you."

"I hate talking about me." Amanda brightened. "Do you like to dance?"

"Never been good at it."

"Me, neither."

Other couples were on the floor, moving slowly, swaying.

"Then I'd like to step on your toes," said Stevens, getting up, and offering his hand. Walking to the dance floor, his fingers locked with hers, a prelude for the rest of the evening.

They danced to a few slow songs, said little, but enjoyed the closeness of each other's touch. They kissed just as the music changed to a rowdy rendition of "Cotton-eyed Joe" and the dance floor filled with two-steppers stomping their feet.

It felt like only moments later when they were under the sheets of her bed. Stevens held her close while she slept, his arm around her, her leg draped over his. For the first time since his wife died, he felt happy and safe. But he knew the feeling wouldn't last.

CHAPTER TWENTY-SEVEN

Stevens blinked, stretched his arm across the bed, and was confused. What day was it? And where was he? Within seconds, the aroma of coffee tickled his nose and he took a breath, realizing he'd spent the night with Amanda.

Now, he felt like Cinderella after the Ball and the old way of life returned when the clock struck midnight. His clothes were on the floor in a heap.

"You awake?" Amanda stood in the doorframe in a tank top just reaching her thighs.

"Yeah." Stevens yawned.

"How do you like your coffee?"

"In a mug."

"Cute."

"Black, like me." He felt glued to the bed. "And the stronger the better."

"Got a cup coming right up."

"I'll be right there," he called after her, yawning and fighting grogginess.

He needed to get going so he could get on with the day and, who knew what. He stretched, got up, and pulled on his jeans and T-shirt. *Damn.* Adrenaline had been fueling his body and now it was depleted.

Stevens staggered into the kitchen, took a seat at the small table, and fought to clear his mind. Amanda was cooking eggs and bacon.

A laptop was open and Stevens caught a headline on the screen: *Is the president safe?*

"You're really worn out," said Amanda, setting a mug in front of him, and turning back to the stove. "Don't worry about reading the article. It raises a hypothetical of the president being assassinated by a sniper." She sighed, grabbed her coffee, and sat. "Reality rears its ugly head."

"Yeah, it sure does."

"Could a sniper really take out the president?"

"I guess. But no reason to with him, he's pretty feckless." Stevens sipped his coffee and frowned. *Oops. No politics. Otherwise, time to leave.*

Amanda saw his expression. "Oh, okay. Not really breakfast talk, huh?" She handed him a plate of eggs, bacon, and a bagel.

"No, not really."

"As you said last night, let's not talk about current events."

"What do you want to talk about?" asked Stevens, smiling.

"You, for a moment anyway. I enjoyed our little date."

"Me, too." Stevens could see questions in Amanda's eyes.

"So, I hate to be so forward, but are you seeing anyone?" she asked.

"Yes."

"Oh."

Stevens smiled. "I'm looking at her right now."

"Cute."

"Aren't you eating?"

"I had some fruit before you got up. That'll be enough for now. I'll probably eat an early lunch when I run errands."

Stevens dug into his eggs. "I'm not really good at this whole dating thing. Actually, I haven't been on a date in years. I don't want to sound desperate or clingy and, I should just shut up now. This is getting awkward, but I'd like to go out with you again, no question."

What the hell am I saying?

Stevens couldn't help himself and continued on. "I wish my work wasn't so crazy, but if you're flexible then we can work around my schedule."

"And mine, too." Amanda sipped her coffee. "I work from here two or three days a week, like today, so lunch or dinner is possible. Starting to like working from home. The commute to the office is a killer."

"I can imagine." He was tempted to eat quickly but forced himself to go slowly.

"So, what are your plans today?" she asked. "Maybe between my errands and whatever you're doing we can…hang out?"

"Wow. Lunch, dinner, and hang out."

Amanda blushed.

"Hey, no blushing," he joked. "I got some admin work, clean up some accounts. But after that—"

"Ah, there ain't no work like paperwork," said Amanda.

Stevens smiled between bites. "That's cute."

"I just made it up."

Damn, she was pleasant.

"Clever. I like your energy," said Stevens, finishing breakfast.

"And yours is quite good, too."

"It's nice to have someone to be *energetic* with," he said, winking and finishing his coffee.

"In a hurry?"

Stevens slowed down. "Not really. I mean, my paperwork can wait." His mind was still racing. "Have you ever been in a car, speeding along, and then you slam on the brakes?"

"Yeah."

"The car stops but your body jolts forward?"

"And where are you going with this analogy?"

"Well, I feel like I'm moving so fast, and you're about to slam on the brakes—"

"And you're scared that you're going to slam your head on the dashboard?" asked Amanda.

"Yeah."

"Then buckle up and wear a seat belt." She laughed. "No, I understand. I feel that way too, but no worries, my foot's not even near the brake pedal."

Stevens smiled, reached over, and held her hand. "Whew, that's a relief." But he knew it wasn't. He knew he was trying to fool himself into believing he could have a normal life. He knew—

Amanda squeezed his hand. "Earth to Bob. Earth to Bob. You there?"

"Oh, sorry. Just lost in thought for a moment."

"A good thought I hope."

"Definitely," he lied.

"Well, if your paperwork can wait, my errands can wait, and we could just, um," she smiled and motioned with her eyes back toward her bedroom, "go back to bed for a while."

Don't get distracted. Don't get involved. Ah, one more time. Stevens grinned, "I like the way you think."

CHAPTER TWENTY-EIGHT

Kilbraide was tired of the spartan bedroom and was longing for his apartment in Hollywood with shirts piled on a chair, socks on the living room floor, and cold beer going lonely in the refrigerator. But home wasn't getting any closer. Now he was summoned to another part of the complex known as the Command Center, a heavily guarded area a few stories underground from where the main surveillance activities occurred.

Monitors glowed while data tech operators processed the information coming across their screens. Biometric images from cameras used for spying on civilians were pouring in from around the country and turning up nothing. Filters used to patrol the internet and sniff out data consisting of massive amounts of "1s" and "0s" captured screenshots of private text and voice messages looking for Red Flags. Still nothing. Stevens had gone to ground.

"We're double-checking social media." Catalonia's eyes were busy. "You think he might have an account somewhere? Maybe on Zudder or ProfileScene under an assumed name?"

Kilbraide replied curtly, "I doubt it. Not his style. But if he did, he certainly wouldn't be using his real name or posting any pictures. But I never had a chance to ask him about it."

The only times Kilbraide had gotten close to Stevens was when he was hunting him in LA for other killings. They got into a fistfight in a home that Stevens was renting and Kilbraide lost, got knocked out, and was stuffed in a hiding place. He had to wait nearly twenty-four hours before being found. They weren't memories that he wanted to relive.

"What side of the bed did you wake up on?"

"The wrong side, I'm starting to believe," said Kilbraide.

"Where the hell is he?" Catalonia kept searching the database. "I thought sociopaths liked to subtly take credit for their destructive deeds, you know, like arsonists. Returning to the scene."

"That's for sociopaths who are really whacked out. Snipers prefer anonymity. No credit needed. No, Stevens sees himself on a covert mission."

"Like a soldier?" she asked.

"Like the soldier he is."

Catalonia smiled. "That's another reason I got you involved."

"What? You think I'm a sociopath?"

"Since you mentioned it."

Kilbraide was annoyed at her banter. "No, I didn't mention it."

"Do you need some coffee, wanna' take a break, go for another run on the taxpayer's dollar? What?"

"I want to do my job as a detective back in LA. I don't want to be here. I just want this to be over and to go home."

Catalonia's smile faded. "You sound like a fuckin' two-year old. Waa, waa. Do your job and this will be over."

"You mean assassinate somebody?"

"Kill a killer and protect Americans. Do your job, so I can do mine."

"And what is your job?"

Catalonia scanned the monitor. "Protecting and serving the people of the United States in every way imaginable with every resource I can get my hands on. So we can avoid utter chaos. Like what's going on right now." She studied the monitor.

"What?"

"This chatter."

Kilbraide looked alongside Catalonia at a news report saying the president was honoring the memories of Schallum, Brae, and Alanasian as heroes of the First Amendment while Congressional leaders stood with him in the Rose Garden. *We can't let heroes of free speech and democracy die in vain, no matter which side we believe they represent. We must all be allowed to speak up and freely speak out.* We must unite our country again."

"Yeah, blah, blah. Just the same old, same old," Kilbraide sighed.

"The guy's an idiot. I didn't vote for him," grumbled Catalonia. "But he's still the president and it's my duty, no, *our* duty to protect him, his followers, and the American public, no matter how weak a leader he is."

Another feed surfaced on her monitor.

"Look at this. Social media's going nuts."

Prez is coward.

Weak. Puppet.

He loved Schallum. She only asked him scripted questions.

'So much for uniting the country," said Kilbraide.

President meeting lawmakers … both sides.

Says Schallum a hero? Bullshit.

Brae wanted one world government.

Send the president packing. Says to ban guns. Disarm extremists like white supremacists.

"The rhetoric's getting old," sighed Catalonia." The usual regurgitation of opinions and rebuttals. To be honest, I actually feel bad for the president, he's in a tough situation."

"Sometimes I really don't get you."

"What's to get?"

Kilbraide explained. "You just called him an idiot, and not for the first time. But now you're sympathizing with him. I don't get you. I mean, where do you stand politically?"

"Let's get this straight, my political leanings don't matter. And neither do yours. Just like your precious LAPD, our job is to serve and protect."

"Okay. One more question," said Kilbraide. "It seems that the president has come into our conversation a few times now. Am I missing something? Do you think he's a target for Stevens?"

"That's two questions and the president's always a target."

"No. Stevens is a military man, patriot to the core—"

"Who kills Americans."

"And your *precious* little Black Ops here doesn't?" said Kilbraide.

"You're bugging the shit out of me. It sounds like you're starting to sympathize with Stevens."

"No, but—"

"No *buts*. Do your job. Find Stevens and kill him."

CHAPTER TWENTY-NINE

Stevens washed the coffee mug with a soapy rag and noticed water dripping from the faucet. "That was good coffee. I like this blend."

"Thanks," said Amanda, sitting at the kitchen table. "Got it at the General Store."

"Really?"

"There's this great coffee roasting company in town."

"I'll try them out," said Stevens.

"Yeah, I get a small bag whenever I go."

"You go often?"

"Just when I run out of coffee."

"Pick me up a bag." Stevens fiddled with the faucet. "You need a new washer on this thing."

"I keep meaning to fix it, but I keep forgetting."

"It doesn't drive you nuts?"

"It does, but I just ignore it."

Stevens unscrewed the faucet and examined it. He showed the rubbery ring to Amanda. "Got any extras?"

"On the back porch."

He headed to the porch while she opened her laptop. "While you're doing that, I'm going to check a few emails."

"Go ahead," said Stevens as he looked on the metal shelving that Amanda had installed. Plastic boxes were neatly labeled *screws*, *electrical*, *plumbing*. Smart woman. The washer was deep inside the plumbing box.

Stevens' smartphone vibrated in his pocket. The feeling of domestic bliss faded as he pulled it out and saw the message.

Status?

He replied, *Here*. Proof that he wasn't a free man. He grabbed the washer and walked back to the kitchen faucet.

Amanda picked up her phone, tapped the screen, and smiled.

"Whatcha' happy about?" asked Stevens.

"Our date at the bar. Inexpensive, but just fun. And, yes, in case you're wondering, I'm one of those who puts up pictures of their meals on Instagram, ProfileScene, Zudder—all of them. And, of course, memorable dates like the one with you."

"You posted our picture?"

"Yeah. Not just one. You don't mind, do you?"

"No, of course not." He forced a smile and looked at the screen. "Oh, yeah, we look nice."

Stevens wasn't online anywhere, until now. He had always stayed invisible with no internet presence. He had gotten so caught up with her that he got sloppy. This was a problem.

"No, we look *cute* together." Amanda laughed. "Hey, Bob, I hate to ask you—"

"Oh, ask me anything."

"We're low on, uh, I mean I'm low on milk. I'm going to be stuck on this project for a while. If you're going to be out today, could you pick up a quart?"

Stevens fit the washer inside the nozzle, wondering how long he had now, how long before Kilbraide was knocking on his door. *Damned social media.* "You mean, pick up some milk?"

"Yeah, if it's convenient."

Stevens walked to where she was on the laptop and felt concerns he had never experienced before. Was Amanda safe? "Milk, huh?"

"Yes, milk," she laughed. "You know, it comes from cows."

"Sure, be glad to." His phone vibrated.

"Client call?"

"Client notification." Stevens glanced at the screen. *You're compromised.* His fears were realized. Those damn selfies. "Oh, sorry. I got to take this. I got to run. I'll grab some milk and be back for dinner."

Amanda smiled. "So you're confirming dinner?"

"Absolutely."

"Sounds good." Amanda stood and kissed Stevens on the lips. "Do you need anything other than milk?"

His phone vibrated again. *Clear out.*

"Persistent client," said Amanda.

"Yeah." Stevens plastered a pleasant look over his worries. Anxiety was wracking his thoughts, and the clock was ticking. He had to leave, now.

"I do need something," she whispered, wrapping an arm around his back. "Smile."

He did, instinctively, as she raised the phone and snapped a selfie.

"Wow, you're certainly quick with that thing," he chuckled, covering his terror. "You going to post that one, too?"

"Of course, and I'll email it to you. You can print it out since you're Old School."

"Okay. I'm afraid to ask, but do you need anything else?"

She playfully nibbled his ear. "Absolutely, and when I do then you'll be the first to know."

He smiled and goose bumps covered his body. "Damn, I love running errands for you."

The phone vibrated again and again.

Amanda furrowed her brow. "Someone really wants you.

"Yeah, let me take this. I'll call you soon." He gave her a quick kiss and headed out the door as he read the message.

Confirm.

Stevens hurried to his cabin with his insides ripping apart. Amanda was incredible, but it was over.

CHAPTER THIRTY

Information overload was a real bitch. Kilbraide, with eyes red and glazed, looked from one data tech to another. He was enclosed in what felt like was a cement hole below the Earth's crust, surrounded with the latest technology. He wanted to be out, scouting around the country. Flying him from one place to another couldn't cost any more than the surveillance geeks tapping on keyboards and living with eye strain.

Data from each region were prioritized: the Bay Area and Los Angeles were designated Region One since Stevens had been a suspected killer in that area. From there, it spread out. Region Two was the mountain states. Region three was the Midwest and Plains states. Region Four was the East Coast, with New York City still hogging the attention.

All these regions farmed data collected from the internet, social media sites, and every email and text messages that users sent. The effort helped track wanted criminals like Stevens but they also infringed on personal liberties that Kilbraide had fought to protect when he enlisted in the army. And who knows who ordered the Command Center built and who was Catalonia's real boss. Who the hell did she work for? Vanguard. Who the hell are they?

Who am I really working for?

How about Stevens? He's working for Black Eagle, but who are they really? Who do they answer to?

So many unknowns weighed on Kilbraide.

He longed for a direct line to Stevens who had called him on a phone that was issued to him. Catalonia and her cronies wasted no time confiscating that phone and issuing Kilbraide another. It would have been helpful to call him back, maybe he'd have answers.

If only it was that easy.

After all, if Stevens was teasing him in Saratoga, then he could tease right back. Kilbraide needed some fresh air. He got up from his surveillance station and took the elevator up a few floors. He emerged on ground level, or Planet Earth as he silently joked.

Stepping outside for real, unfiltered air felt wonderful and when the sun soaked him, Kilbraide realized something. Stevens was an adventurer. Each of the murders that he had committed in Los Angeles a few years ago took place outdoors in some sort of recreational setting: by a swimming pool; on an equestrian trail; a bike path along the beach. It's believed Stevens was offshore bobbing on a jet ski when he took down a wealthy businesswoman who was on a morning jog on the boardwalk.

Yeah, he once had an office in North Hollywood but that was a façade. Stevens thrived on the outdoors and was waging guerilla warfare with his kill-and-run tactics. He wasn't a Mafioso-type pulling up to gun people down in their neatly pressed suits. Taking out such high-profile figures was going for maximum exposure and sending a message: if you step outside the law, harm others, you'll pay the price, and die when you least expect it.

Kilbraide figured it was the ultimate Fuck Around and Find Out, maybe a motto in Stevens' mind. Fuck around with the freedoms and liberties allowed in America and you'll find out what happens.

Kilbraide picked up his cell phone and called Catalonia who answered with her typical why-the-hell-are-you-calling voice.

"What's up?"

God, she was always so friendly. He gathered his thoughts. "Just thinking about Stevens being an outdoorsman."

"So?"

Kilbraide sighed. "So, look in every small mountain town, or tiny beach community. Start in California."

"That narrows it down." Catalonia's sarcasm was hard to take. "Where are you?"

"Outside. I can only suck in stale air for so long."

"Oh, yeah? You live in LA."

"I get to the beach a lot. Listen, we need to look from the Bay Area to Los Angeles. So, it's narrowed."

"Why not Bum-fuck, Texas?"

"That works, too, see you soon." Kilbraide clicked off.

He had an idea while he scrolled through social media platforms: *Mountain town residents, California. Outdoor people, Bay Area.* Thousands of posts dating back to the invention of the internet turned up. Searching each one was going to consume one hour after another.

Was it worth it?

Kilbraide thought so.

He brought up a map of California that showed him why the state was unique, and a natural sanctuary for quiet killers. San Diego to LA was a megalopolis with urban sprawl from the oceans to the deserts. But just north beyond Ventura to Santa Barbara there were pockets of small hamlets in the mountains.

It was still an enormous area, but the mountains could let someone pivot to the crowded beaches, to the Central Valley, or to Silicon Valley.

Julius Brae. ProfileScene.

ProfileScene was a quick drive in from—where? Commuters. Who commutes to Silicon Valley?

Kilbraide's searches turned up the bedroom community of Modesto. No, not Stevens' type of place. He was a man who liked the earth. Dirt. Danger. Rugged.

Nature that borders Silicon Valley. Santa Cruz Mountains. Redwoods.

Kilbraide's phone buzzed. Catalonia. *Damn her.*

"Joe's Pizza. Mushrooms or anchovies?"

"Cut the shit, I mean it. Get in here. We've got something of interest."

So do I, thought Kilbraide. But no harm in listening to the boss. "Be right there." Kilbraide pocketed the phone and headed to the depths of the Command Center.

CHAPTER THIRTY-ONE

Monitors glowed and techies spoke in hushed tones while scanning. Kilbraide found Catalonia huddled in the center of the quiet buzzing. She motioned him over to where she stood next to a data specialist.

"Nice to have you back from your stretch break."

She annoyed him so badly that he wanted to kill Stevens just to get her out of his life. Hard to believe that he had actually been attracted to her at first. He shook off a chill.

Kilbraide looked at the monitor. "What's up?"

"Facial recognition comes through. Finally."

The image was dark around the edges, an interior shot with two faces lit by backlights. The specialist typed on the keys to enlarge the image.

Kilbraide studied the setting. Wood-grain walls and the first four letters of *Budweiser* were in the background. Definitely a bar. "It's him."

"Yeah." Catalonia compared the image on a bank of monitors to the right showing Stevens in the SunRise America TV studio where he toured and got Schallum's autograph.

"Who's the woman?" Kilbraide was puzzled and knew about the past heartbreak that Stevens suffered over his wife. How'd the photo get taken? A casual acquaintance?

"Looks like a friend of Stevens. Posted this all over social media but didn't say anything special." The tech and others around him were busy typing on one key after another. The hot lead kicked the whole operation into a frenzy.

Data bank after data bank of images scrolled through.

"Got a match," yelled one.

Catalonia and Kilbraide hurried to the workstation. The image was a woman sitting at a laptop with colleagues in an office with floor-to-ceiling windows and office furniture in pastel colors. Across her desk was a banner, *Happy Birthday*.

This and other photos linked to her profile on Instagram, ProfileScene.com and Zudder.com, among others. Key information was there. A first and last name. Amanda Richelieu. Her general location was *Santa Cruz Mountains*.

"I was right. California. Bay Area. More or less," said Kilbraide.

"Don't let it go to your head," remarked Catalonia.

"She's divorced," said an operator. "Mid-30s."

There were other pictures of her with Stevens in a cozy home setting, using pliers on a faucet in the background while Amanda smiled and sipped coffee taking selfies.

"She doesn't have a clue," said Kilbraide.

"What do you mean?" Catalonia scrolled through more images.

Another tech spoke up. "She doesn't have any kids. Works for Zudder.com."

"The social media site? Jesus," exclaimed Kilbraide. "Is that why he's with her? Getting close to another target?" Kilbraide looked at more photos. Each one was casual and candid. "She has no idea who he is. Quite the selfie-taker, though."

The floodgate opened and the operators continued finding new information and more images. Amanda shopping in an outdoor mall with another woman. Sitting at a café, wearing what looked like a warm running outfit.

Must have been chilly. Definitely Bay Area.

He had the tech zoom in to see what looked like a trendy shopping district.

More images cascaded onto the screen with one that piqued Kilbraide's interest. Thick trees.

Catalonia scanned another monitor. They were all just happy-go-lucky, personal moments.

Another image surfaced with her back to a cabin that was surrounded by plenty of leafy vegetation and what looked like redwood trees. The setting was California.

A man was in the background but he was looking off to the side and he wasn't posed for the picture. Like he didn't know it was being taken.

"Zoom in," said Kilbraide.

"There's hundreds," Catalonia countered.

"No, zoom in on this one. On the man."

The tech operator typed the keys and the image expanded. He pressed a few more keys and cleaned it up as much as technology would allow.

Paydirt.

Each image confirmed it was Stevens.

Another candid shot rolled across the screen: Stevens climbing into a truck.

"Thank you, Amanda," muttered Kilbraide. "You're a wealth of knowledge. Sometimes you gotta' love social media."

He turned to Catalonia. "I can tell it's the mountains near the Bay Area."

The tech rolled his eyes and called out, "Yeah, the GPS coordinates are embedded in every picture. Look here, genius. We've got her address."

"Alright, let's scramble a team," ordered Catalonia.

"Am I good or what?" Kilbraide smiled at her.

"Yeah, I would go with the 'what' part. Why are you standing there? Get going."

The woman was all heart. Certainly, one that was incredibly icy.

***

Stevens was inside his cabin trying to think but his heart was pounding. Clear out. What would he take? What would he leave? Was this permanent or would he be coming back? Dumb question. He'd never be coming back. His phone vibrated. Amanda texted the photo she had just taken of them. Heart emojis framed the image. He smiled but wanted to cry at the same time as reality kicked in.

Shit.

Breadcrumbs all over the internet. Any brainiac whiz kid could track him down so how long before a kill squad showed up? Unbelievable.

Ripping himself away from Amanda seemed impossible. He had to leave. He didn't want her in danger. Time was running out. Stevens felt like he was trapped inside an hourglass and someone had turned it upside down and the sand was pouring from top to bottom, suffocating him.

His phone vibrated, but his hands were shaking as badly as his insides. The vibrating wouldn't quit until he finally steadied himself and saw the text.

Assignment. Salt Lake City. Confirm.

Stevens was stunned. *You've got to be kidding me. Now?*

Panic gripped him like he was a rag doll, tossing him from one room to another while he wondered what he'd pack—not just to leave, but for a new assignment. The thought of a cleaning crew coming through after he left made him choke.

No. That wasn't going to happen. He'd figured it out and be back.

Another message hit.

Confirm.

Stevens dashed back into his bedroom, moved a throw rug, and lifted a trapdoor. Personal mementos and his cache of weapons. The rifle that was so familiar.

He lifted his phone, stared at the screen, and took a breath. Bad timing, but duty calls. *Confirming.*

CHAPTER THIRTY-TWO

The driver of a bright red CJ-5 Jeep emblazoned with the county's Fire Team logos on the doors lurched over ruts, crawling up the old fire road, maneuvering around large rocks and fallen branches. Bud Moore thought nothing of the jostling, but Kilbraide's lower back made a lousy suspension system as he rode in the front passenger seat. He was armed with his 9mm service pistol tucked away comfortably in a shoulder holster beneath his ghillie suit, custom camouflaged to blend in with the mountain environment. His rifle and other gear, concealed in a canvas backpack, lay across the small back seat.

The old jeep crawled over another fallen limb, bouncing Kilbraide in his seat.

"Dude, seriously, you could have avoided that one," Kilbraide moaned.

"Why? It'd take all the fun out of doing a little four-wheeling."

"And you couldn't have just dropped me off near the main road?"

"Too conspicuous." Moore jerked the steering wheel right and then left.

"As if this bright red jeep isn't?"

"We're just the fire crew keeping the road clear. Your tax dollars at work."

Moore hit another rock.

"Well, you're doing a lousy job of it." Kilbraide glanced from the woods to the road.

"For being an ex-Ranger sniper, you sure are a candy-ass."

The road split off into a small clearing surrounded by trees with branches high above blocking out whatever sun broke through the late afternoon clouds. The driver turned into the clearing and hit the brakes.

Kilbraide looked at him. "What's up?"

"End of the road." Moore pointed to the GPS unit mounted on the dashboard. "This is where you get out. You gotta' hoof it from here."

Kilbraide looked around. "Here?"

"Here. This is your evac spot." Moore laned back, kicked his feet up, and pulled his hat over his eyes. "I'll be waiting."

"Damn, I was just getting used to your horrible driving."

Moore peeked out from under his hat. "You're still here? Going to be dark soon. Go that way." He pointed to a jagged game trail that disappeared quickly into the heavily wooded forest, then pulled the hat back over his eyes.

Kilbraide climbed out of the Jeep, grabbed the pack out of the back, and slung it over his shoulder as he headed toward the trail.

"Happy hunting, pansy."

"Maybe I'll take the easy way back and call an Uber."

Kilbraide entered the woods and followed the game trail down the mountain until it faded. During the flight to California, he had studied the area based on municipal maps and satellite images. He pulled out his pocket GPS, did a quick survey of the area, then made his way deeper into the dense trees.

He hiked through the forest, focusing on the task at hand. He loved this part, being in nature, the smell of moss growing on the sides of trees. Hard to believe that this area was as out of the way as possible while still being close to a major urban center.

Just as the sun was setting, he arrived at a tree line overlooking a gentle slope that led down to Amanda's cabin two hundred yards below.

Kilbraide blended into the surrounding forest, concealing himself behind fallen logs. He opened his pack and started preparing his gear. He thought about the outcome – taking another life. He hated that part. He finished assembling his rifle, attaching the scope, suppressor, and bipod.

Catalonia's voice interrupted the silence of his thoughts, exploding in his earpiece, "Status?"

He certainly didn't want to deal with her now and curtly whispered back, "In position."

"Target?"

Kilbraide looked through the rangefinder at the cabin below. The sun had set and the cabin was dimly lit with a porch light and a bulb in the kitchen. "Dark. No movement."

"Keep me informed."

"Will do." Kilbraide waited. A breeze rustled leaves and birds sounded in the distance. He could tell Catalonia's mic was still active. After another moment of dead air, she spoke solemnly.

"Kilbraide. We can't have any more fuck-ups. Don't hesitate. If target is acquired at location, you have permission to engage."

"Noted."

Catalonia clicked off.

Kilbraide picked up the rangefinder and scanned the cabin and surrounding area again. He confirmed what he already knew from the maps, drones, and satellite images. Beyond Amanda's cabin and on either side, there were other seasonal cabins and year-round homes. Most were spaced about an acre or two apart. He could see lights coming on in some of them. Families and people getting away from the city were enjoying their time in the mountains.

He studied Amanda's cabin again, her driveway, her porch, even her chicken coop out back. He suspected she was an innocent and he didn't want her to become collateral damage. It nagged him that she may have to witness Stevens' death.

Kilbraide rehearsed going through the motions and finding the optimal place to take Stevens out. If Stevens even showed up. He formulated and went over his backup plan, Plan B, and his egress to evac.

Through the trees to the left of Amanda's cabin was another cabin. But unlike the others in the area this one was completely dark, not even a porch light. There was no movement and no signs that anybody even lived there. Probably just a weekend getaway.

Kilbraide's stomach growled. *Time for dinner.*

He broke into his field rations, eating a power-bar, drinking from a water bladder, then settled in for what could be a long night.

He listened to the sound of coyotes howling in the distance and crickets chirping for love. He finally started to relax when headlights appeared on the road leading to Amanda's cabin. Adrenaline shot through his veins as he got in position, shouldered the rifle, and looked through the riflescope to trail the movement of the car.

Kilbraide keyed his mic. "We have movement."

Catalonia wasted no time replying. "What do ya' got?"

"Late model sedan pulling into the drive."

"Stay frosty."

"Seriously? Did you just say that? Come on, enough with the cliches." He watched as the car stopped, reversed out of the driveway, and backed onto the street. "Hold."

"Update?"

"Looks like a false alarm. Maybe wrong address."

The car continued past Amanda's cabin then slowed and turned into the driveway of the dark cabin next door, stopping near the porch. Kilbraide watched intently as a woman, leaving the headlights on, got out of the car and walked toward the front door.

"Kilbraide, status update?"

"Hold."

The woman stepped into the beam of the headlights and Kilbraide could instantly see that it was Amanda Richelieu. She walked up to the dark cabin, knocked, and waited. No answer. She knocked again, then retreated into her car and backed down the driveway.

"Amanda just knocked on the cabin next door. Nobody home," said Kilbraide.

"What're your thoughts?"

"Not sure."

Kilbraide watched her drive back to her own cabin, park, and then enter with an armful of groceries, turning on the lights inside. She was acting so damned normal, just like she looked in the pictures with Stevens and that gave Kilbraide an idea.

"Give me some background on the cabin next door. Names? Who owns it? Rented? Leased? Whatever you got."

He heard Catalonia barking orders to her assistants while he surveyed the landscape.

She got back to him quickly. "Working on it. Stand by. Any sign of Stevens?"

Kilbraide looked through the riflescope and watched Amanda move from room to room inside the cabin, putting groceries away. He felt like a voyeur. "No sign at all."

"You know, Kilbraide. Sometimes you have good ideas. Real genius. I got something for you. The cabin is owned by a corporation named Franklin Industries, which is a subsidiary of Parker

Communications, owned by Freedom Technologies. Rented to, leased to, blah blah blah… It's a shell. You know what that means?"

"Stevens."

"Bingo! Relocate your position."

"No. I have a clear line on both cabins."

"Your call. Keep me updated."

"Roger."

Catalonia said something out of character before clicking off: "Don't call me Roger."

Kilbraide shook his head and smiled at the bad pun. For the moment, he was relieved that he didn't have to take a life.

During the next couple of hours, he watched as Amanda did chores, ate dinner, and then turned off the lights in the cabin, one by one, to finally settle in bed and open a book. She only read for a few minutes before clicking off the light and curling up under the covers.

It was a nice night. Everything was peaceful. Kilbraide rolled onto his back, took in the majesty of the stars above, and thought about how this shit was getting old. He had dealt with this enough during his tours of duty. He was already tired and just wanted to go back to LA, sleep in his own bed, and get away from all this espionage and spy crap.

His earpiece squawked with Catalonia's voice. "Abort mission. Head to evac immediately."

"Wait, what?"

"Stand down. Facial recognition just picked up Stevens at a few different locations. He's headed to Salt Lake."

"Salt Lake City?"

"Yeah, he's driving a pick-up truck. The one we saw in the photo. Spotted him at a truck stop outside of Reno getting gas."

"How do you know where he's heading?"

"He keeps driving east on I-80."

"But why Salt Lake?"

"Zudder.com. Zach Price, you know Amanda's big boss. Well, he's making an appearance there in a few days."

"Jesus. Sounds familiar."

"It gets better. The president is scheduled to speak. Supposed to give some type of humanitarian-free speech award to Price."

"Free speech award? You're kidding? To Price? Don't make me laugh. He's worse than Brae. Zudder's fact-checkers censor everybody that doesn't agree with his New World Order view."

"Regardless. Get to evac. Your ride's waiting."

The line went dead before he could respond.

Kilbraide looked through his riflescope, scanning the area one last time. Amanda was sound asleep in her bed. Everything was quiet. He turned toward what he now believed was Stevens' cabin. Still dark. Nobody was there.

He broke down his rifle, packed his gear, and headed back into the woods, dreading the return ride down the mountain in the old Jeep. Kilbraide got about a hundred yards before he stopped and turned back to look at Stevens' cabin. The detective in him knew that he had to check it out. He pulled off his ghillie suit, stashed his backpack, checked his sidearm, and stealthily made his way to the cabin.

He went around the perimeter checking windows and doors, thankful there were no motion-sensor lights or alarms. Kilbraide came back to the front door and turned the knob. Locked. Knowing that it would be too easy, he tried anyway and ran his fingers along the top sill of the door frame. No key. He looked under the mat. No key. He decided that he needed to break a window and climb in.

Kilbraide went to a side window, smashed the glass with his elbow, reached through, unlocked and slid the window up. He felt like a two-bit criminal as he climbed into the darkness of the cabin and turned on his penlight.

The inside was quaint but definitely had the look of a man's home, no feminine touches. He searched cautiously around. Nothing out of the ordinary. The place was orderly, but still looked as if someone had left in a hurry. A few coats were scattered, a cabinet left open, and dishes in the sink. He opened the refrigerator and found a six-pack of craft beer enticing him.

Why the hell not?

He grabbed a bottle, twisted off the top, and took a healthy swig. Not his favorite, but not bad. He set the beer on the counter and noticed that it was the same brand that Stevens had bought for him in Saratoga Springs. This was definitely Stevens' place.

Kilbraide went into the dark bedroom. It had the same feel with drawers left open and clothes scattered on the bed. Nothing of interest and nothing to actually tie Stevens here, except for the craft beer. He turned to leave but his foot caught on a small throw rug. He slid it aside to find a trapdoor embedded in the floor.

Bingo!

Kilbraide checked the door for booby traps and alarms and finding nothing, he lifted it. Inside he saw empty foam cut-outs of where weapons, ammunition, and other gear would have been stored. Aside from that, the space looked empty.

His earpiece erupted with Catalonia's voice. "Status. Evac's waiting."

"Had to check something out. On the way."

He went to close the trapdoor when he noticed what looked like a scrap of paper sticking out from beneath a piece of the foam. He lifted it and found personal mementos from Stevens' life. Postcards, writings that looked like letters, passports with different names, and credit cards.

Kilbraide caught his breath. There was a poster of a Marine sergeant from the early 1900s known as the *fightingest* Marine ever. It was the same poster he had seen previously in Stevens' North Hollywood office.

And there it was—a hard copy photo of Stevens and his deceased wife and another of Stevens and Amanda. The same one that she had recently posted on Zudder.com. They both looked happy, and that was sad because it wasn't going to be a happy ending.

Kilbraide fought his instincts. As a detective, he would have immediately gathered the items but with the situation as unique as it was, and Stevens being who he was, he decided to use his phone and snap photos of the evidence.

CHAPTER THIRTY-THREE

The Olympic Park's glory days had arrived and vanished in mere weeks. The park and other venues built for the 2002 Winter Olympics became a testament of American resolve after the tragedy of 9/11. But that was ancient history and that energy of decades earlier was confined inside a museum. On the outside, the ski jumps and bobsled runs were a tourist attraction with a zip line and plenty of locations to snap selfies. It was a family-friendly outdoor stop between Salt Lake City and Park City at an area known as The Junction.

Zach Price saw the need to bring America together again after the recent killings had pushed the nation's rhetoric in a direction that wound the tension tighter than ever. Law enforcement across the country and the FBI seemed paralyzed and unable to stop a form of odd, guerilla warfare that targeted leaders on the left, including Julius Brae who had been classmates with him in the computer science program during their undergrad years. Price believed he was taking the *high road* by quietly sharing his vision with the White House. Critics decried his views as the engineering of a socialist utopia, but Price believed it was the best way forward for America. The thoughts stirred his own curiosity about seeking the presidency.

The venue was set and in just a few days, the chosen location, a new amphitheater built in the heart of The Junction, would be filled with American flags flapping beneath mostly blue skies while the surrounding Wasatch Mountains stood guard. Price convinced the White House that Salt Lake was bustling as a new technological center that was in harmony with the environment. Professionals of all political persuasions worked alongside each other and were proof that business and nature—as well as people—could coexist.

***

A hiking trail wound from the park into the mountains and gradually rose in elevation until the setting below looked like a sandbox filled with toys. Few hikers used the trail beyond the third mile marker. The ones who did were runners or mountaineers in excellent condition and they didn't blaze their own paths at this point but followed the trail markings.

No one would think to look or explore a half-mile off the trail shrouded in brush where Bob Stevens was dug in between boulders. Scratches on his arms and one along his neck were proof that he had found a well-protected hide that would discourage curious trailblazers.

His binoculars helped him see details in the park and beyond its borders to the outlet malls, condos, and all locations where the Secret

Service would post sharpshooters for the president's visit. Security details were already gathering in the area, and on the day of the event helicopters would be hovering with extra eyes to safeguard the president and other dignitaries. Stevens smirked. The area he chose was high enough that he'd be eye level with the choppers, or just above them.

News reports would simply say the president was in Utah giving Zach Price a bullshit humanitarian award, but there'd be no mention of the hundreds of man-hours of preparation crammed into just a few days. No one would see the frenzy of the Secret Service agents or the low-level staffers who sweated every detail. TV viewers would only see two men who had everything completely under control.

The wind was one of the variables that could ruin the shot, so Stevens took precautions. He set up his miniature Kestrel weather station on a portable camping table with a canvas top to measure wind flow, humidity, and other factors.

He picked up his binoculars again and zoomed in on the amphitheater. Intel showed the seating arrangements of the local dignitaries. Mayors and elected officials from around the state would either be on the stage to rub shoulders with Price and the president, or they'd be peering up from the front row. Utah was quite rural, so the president arriving was big news and everyone who was anyone, or wanted to be anyone, was ready to appear at the event.

Mountains don't simply slope from top to bottom. They're uneven with rises and dips, much like life. Stevens dug a small trench, one shovelful after another, piling up the excess dirt like a berm. No rest after the twelve-hour drive.

He cut weeds and thin tree branches from the surrounding spruce and fir trees to cover the embankment. He was excavating his temporary home that would obscure him and his equipment.

Experience taught him to conceal his presence as much as possible, like preparing a latrine to hide any odor from his waste. No need to make it easy if a K-9 patrol took to the hills. He also shoveled a flat platform to lie prone, look through his riflescope during the event, and choose the best angle. Everything hinged on this shot, but Stevens didn't feel any pressure. Every other concern was floating away, and he was entering an almost blissful state where there were no other concerns close to him.

None. Absolutely none.

Stevens settled on the mountainside and unhooked his cell phone from the solar charger. Time to play games and pass the hours. He gazed over the valley and wondered. One text wouldn't hurt. He decided to send a simple *Thinking of you* message to Amanda, but when he powered up his cell there were multiple text messages from her.

Hey there.

Where are you? You really rushed out.

Are you okay? Hope you're doing well.

Call when you can. You're a great cuddle bunny.

Miss you.

He froze as her words overshadowed his purpose for being on the mountain. It didn't even occur to Stevens that this was going to rank as one of the longest shots ever made, almost four thousand yards. Hearing from Amanda was more important. *Shit.* Fury and disappointment hit along with an anger and unhappiness that he couldn't block her out of his thoughts, so he replied. *Sorry. An emergency came up with a client out of state. I'll call soon. Miss you, too.*

He set the phone aside and began to contemplate his purpose. A precise shot required precise thinking. Focus was essential.

People didn't exist so therefore problems didn't exist. His only task was to eliminate his target. Life was much simpler thinking that way. The only option was a successful mission, so why worry that it wouldn't happen?

Stevens checked the mountain and the ravines for his exit. He memorized the terrain, checked the weather reports, and determined how strong the airflow would be as the temperature rose and dipped throughout the day.

He knelt in the trench, loving the feel of dirt on his knees and pressed his chest against the berm. The binoculars showed people and equipment below. It was going to be a big day in Utah's history. Stevens was going within himself in a wonderful way. His thoughts were now consumed with the elimination, and he ran through the checklist.

He rehearsed the morning and the moment over and over again. It would go perfectly as expected. Zach Price needed to go and that's exactly what would happen.

CHAPTER THIRTY-FOUR

Kilbraide strode onto the amphitheater's stage with enough authority that none of the workers questioned his presence. *Act like you belong.* He needed enough time to conduct line of sight reconnaissance, measuring distances to the surrounding areas. There were few options. Condos were at an impossible angle even for a marksman like Stevens. Buildings in the nearby outlet mall weren't very tall, plus Secret Service personnel were already crawling over every inch.

The best option for a long-range sniper was one that Kilbraide couldn't believe. He scanned the brush-strewn foothills and wondered. Stevens was the same guy who held world-record shots while serving in the Marines.

Kilbraide had earlier studied the route from the airport, the location of Price's office, and how the president would arrive. The Secret Service offered protection against the typical crazed assassin who lurked within immediate range of the president. Any kook who tried something would get toasted.

Stevens had nothing ordinary about him. He wouldn't be in any of the places that the Secret Service would expect. Terrorists and assassins craved notoriety and attention. But Stevens was a professional and knew his job was to stay invisible. He liked striking quietly and, as Catalonia revealed, had the support to do so. He pursued his craft—mayhem with a long-range rifle.

The stage was set and time was ticking on what would be a simple stop for the president who was on his way to Seattle for a private $5,000 per plate fundraising dinner and an Asian-American economic summit. If all went well, then Price would head back to his office to see how he could further chip away at free speech in America.

An alert hit Kilbraide's phone. More facial recognition of Stevens in the Salt Lake area.

Catalonia followed with a phone call. "Anything to report?"

"No."

"Keep me updated."

"Will do." Kilbraide hung up and decided to measure distances from the event to the surrounding points of interest. Nothing made sense. There was no clear line of fire from anywhere where a sniper would normally be, and this left Kilbraide with a dilemma. Again, not knowing where Stevens would be, or even pinpointing a general area, meant he couldn't choose his own hide. Frustration struck.

In the military, Kilbraide knew where his target would be and had plenty of ground and air support to back him. Working nearly alone like this was madness. As a detective, he followed clues and hunted down suspects, but he did it with a team he could work with and not a team who threatened his life, like the one he's being forced to work with now. It seemed like Kilbraide's only hope was that Stevens would mess up at some point. His cover would get blown, or he'd be eliminated by his own people. *If* he was arrested and tossed in jail then guaranteed, before any court date, they'd find him hanging in his cell and the CCTV camera would've malfunctioned. Or, mysteriously, he'd just disappear from the jail, never to be seen again.

Kilbraide kept teasing himself about walking off the job. People would forget about Julius Brae and Marcia Schallum since there were other geniuses and loudmouths popping up every day to make our lives easier through technology while spouting their elitist opinions.

All he had to do was phone Catalonia and tell her to stick her intel where the *sun don't shine.* He really missed LA and wasn't allowed to get in touch with Detective Stone. His status at the LAPD nagged him like a thorn stuck in his thumb. But what if Catalonia's henchmen came after him? She warned him earlier that he wasn't allowed to fail or walk away. He only had one choice, complete the mission or get disappeared.

How could this be a democracy with all the crazy subterfuge and spy craft?

So back to the task.

Stevens prided himself on unbelievable long-range shots. He was a master at obscuring his position by using nature and blending in with the environment. Kilbraide squinted again up toward the surrounding mountains. *Where in the hell?* He stepped away from the event preparations and studied the maps. Hiking trails wound up from the Olympic Center and covered quite a distance.

That's the only place Stevens could be. So, why not? I could use a hike.

Kilbraide made his way to the trailhead and started walking, slowly gaining elevation, and stopping every few hundred yards to assess distances and possible angles. Brush, rocks, and trees filled the landscape on both sides of the trail. He couldn't see any possible positions even after taking the drone out of the backpack and letting it buzz overhead.

Kilbraide walked beyond the one-mile mark. Same routine. He stopped, checked his instruments. Trudged one way and then the other, nearly twisting his ankle. The drone flew overhead with nothing to show for the effort. The Olympic Village already looked small, but he continued up the trail, climbing higher and reaching the two-mile mark. He pulled out his rangefinder, located the amphitheater below, and could barely see the stage. People definitely looked like ants and little did they know that they were going to get dusted up.

Absolutely no way in hell.

The land looked just as hostile as ever. How many acres were there? So many places to hide. Stevens could be happy living under a rock and waiting. The man had a genius about him, but it was too damned bad his talents were misguided and deadly.

Kilbraide walked off the trail, sat down, looked into the setting sun, and figured a sleepless night was waiting for him. The event was in the morning and he had never felt so defeated in his life.

CHAPTER THIRTY-FIVE

The morning was clear as surveillance choppers hovered over the Olympic Village. A caravan of black SUVs wound up the road, along the curves and fanned out in the parking lot. Price and the president had arrived and encountered the usual type of complaining protesters who mixed with an adoring crowd. The president was making a quick trip but the locals were making the most of the event with live music, craftspeople displaying their goods, and dignitaries droning on and on.

Kilbraide found a spot in the foothills north and east of the village and dug in, camouflaged in his ghillie suit. He launched his drone repeatedly but saw nothing except brush, a few birds, and the gathering crowds below. His rifle was on the ready if he spotted Stevens' hide. He asked Catalonia for support but none was forthcoming. Even Black Ops had limits, red tape, and internal politics to deal with. He was on his own.

He studied the area below and knew from his vantage point that a clear shot would require every bit of skill he was able to muster. Where was Stevens? At a higher or lower elevation? How well could he see his target? Time grew closer and Kilbraide felt like the landscape was swallowing him up.

***

Crosshairs lined up on one speaker, but who it was didn't matter. It's where Price would stand. Stevens was ready to adjust his line of sight. An earpiece linked to his phone let him pick up coverage of the event and listen to the speeches. Elected officials rambled on about regional business growth and their achievements in protecting the environment. Stevens used the monotone blather like white noise to go deep within himself and visualize the shot taking down Price. And then the speeches stopped. Energy picked up as the president and Price entered the stage while an upbeat pop song blared through the speakers.

Stevens peered through the riflescope. He watched and waited with interest. Secret Service personnel kept a tight perimeter. Nothing else mattered. He breathed deeply, locking in on the target. The day was beautiful. Life was beautiful and Price would be dead within the hour.

The cheering crowd was hand-picked with the president's staunchest supporters along with the employees and vendors who wanted Price to grant raises and give them continued business. Positioned in strategic locations throughout the amphitheater were reporters from all major news outlets with pre-approved questions that were friendly to the president and his policies. The president moved to the microphone while Price shook hands with people around him. He sat on the stage with other politicians and celebrities who preached about the environment while nestled in their multi-million-dollar homes around Park City and flew in their private jets to film festivals around the globe. Price was partially obscured but Stevens was willing to wait until he was speaking at the podium. Much more impact.

Stevens squinted through the riflescope then glanced at the anemometer. The wind shifted ever so slightly. He adjusted the windage and elevation knobs on his scope accordingly while the president defined prosperity as a healthy economy with a healthy environment.

"The environment includes the air we breathe, the water we drink, and the land where we live. But it also includes an environment where we share our ideas without fear of reprisal. Let's not contaminate our society with the rhetoric of hatred when we need to cleanse the hatred with respectful commentary. Rather than fight over our disagreements, let's be mature and accept others' points of view." He glanced over at Price who gave him an encouraging nod before continuing. "If we as Americans can embrace opposing views, then we'll be a model of cooperation and civility for other countries around the globe to emulate."

The crowd applauded.

Stevens inhaled and exhaled while listening but ignoring the bullshit paternal attitude.

"I'm proud to say that the great people of Utah are leaders in diversity, tolerance, and the ability to lay differences aside and work as one."

Applause and cheers led to a standing ovation.

"One of the reasons I'm here is to let you know that next week in the White House I'll be hosting a global communication summit where a man you know well will be honored. He represents the very best of hard work, ingenuity, citizenship, and you know him as the creator and founder of Zudder.com, a simple application that opened up the world and changed how we communicate—Zach Price."

Price took the stage with a chorus of cheers while Stevens breathed deeply, relaxing his body on the exhale.

"Thank you, Mr. President. You're the inspiration for the Free People, Free World initiative."

More cheers.

"Your leadership is an inspiration to us all."

The president gave his practiced smile. "You're an inspiration to us as well. Now I'm on my way to the Pacific Rim summit in Seattle, leaving you in good hands. Thank you all."

The president waved as he walked off stage, surrounded by his security detail.

Price addressed the crowd. "A great day, isn't it?"

The wind shifted once more. Stevens did a series of mental calculations while he focused on the target. Price was in the clear. His riflescope showed Price's face smack in the crosshairs and Stevens had a slight pressure on the trigger, but he felt now wasn't the time. Let the man speak and dig his own grave.

Someone in the audience lifted a small child onto the stage and Price picked her up, held her, and rambled on about our commitment to future generations, allowing them to grow up in a world that was unified in thought and action, and how Zudder.com was a leader in intellectual technologies bringing communities together through open communication. And to accomplish this," he continued, "we must stomp out racist and divisive speech whenever and wherever it occurs. And this is why with the help of the president, and the late Senator Alanasian, and Julius Brae we developed and are putting into action the Free People, Free World initiative."

Stevens ignored the diatribe and stayed focused on the task. He knew how to trust instincts and wait.

***

Price lowered the child into waiting arms and began speaking when a reporter shouted a question from the audience.

"What do you say to people who claim you're enforcing restrictions and curtailing freedom?"

The hand-picked audience groaned at the rogue reporter's question, but Price's smug, but confident smile, showed how he had already thought through the issue. "Yes, all the viral hashtags about Zudder.com censoring free speech. I'm sorry, I don't recognize you. Who are you? Who are you with?"

"Carter Blakley, NewsFactsMedia."

"Oh, yes. You guys really push all the conspiracy theories."

The audience laughed as Blakley politely defended the jab. "We push facts which is why I'd like your response."

A smattering of boos rippled through the crowd, but Price motioned for calm. "No, let him talk. This is what Zudder.com is about. An open dialogue."

"Conservatives say that Zudder.com along with ProfileScene are well known for silencing their voices and they fear—"

"Not true."

The reporter continued. "You're continually blocking, deleting accounts, and shadow banning any voice that doesn't agree with your values."

"Again, not true. You seem to have your facts wrong. All accounts have to comply with our community standards."

"I'm sure your fact-checkers would flag me and tell me my facts are wrong – they have done so many times in the past."

The crowd laughed.

"The fact-checkers are independently—" Price countered but the reporter interrupted again.

"Independent organizations created and hired by you with all—"

"Mr. Blakley, I know you have a job to do, but this is going nowhere."

"Your fact-checkers never check the facts of the left. Those blatantly seem to go unchecked whereas, as I was saying earlier… you continually block, and *fact-check*, conservative speech. But your own company's Mission Statement clearly states 'Open Dialogue and Free Speech for All.'"

"And we abide by that," said Price.

"Only if it meets left-wing agenda and ideologies."

The audience groaned.

Price smiled confidently like a parent talking down to a child. "You sound like you're trying to make a name for yourself, but we're going in circles here. Did you have another question? Maybe one about why we're here today?"

"Yes, I have another question. If it is true that Julius Brae was killed because of his extremely biased views and using his platform to promote them, aren't you worried that you're also a target?"

"What happened to my dear friend, Julius, was absolutely horrible. Stop trying to sensationalize everything for ratings."

"I'm not sensationalizing it. Your friend was murdered. That's a fact."

"Look, Mr. Blakley, as we all know, Zudder.com stands for Open Dialogue and Free Speech for All, and I proudly stand behind that – no matter how activists like you try to twist it into something else."

"People want to know that their freedoms are still protected under the Constitution."

Price smiled and responded with a rehearsed answer that his supporters liked. "What is freedom? Isn't it more freeing to know we think as one and move in one common direction? Wouldn't it be great to be free of conflict? Our ability to achieve will be limitless." Price turned to the mountains. "Each person will be like those peaks in the distance towering to the sky."

***

In the exact moment that Price turned, Stevens pulled the trigger and sent the round careening over sagebrush-encrusted ridges and rocks at over three-thousand feet per second, slamming into the tech genius' face and killing him instantly.

Stevens broke down his equipment while counting one-thousand one, one-thousand two, one-thousand three—counting while he reached in a pocket, pulled out his infamous *One Shot, One Kill* patch and set it on a rock for maximum visibility. Then he sent a text: *Done.* And within forty seconds he was gone, leaving his hide intact.

No need to watch the scene unfold. This was all part of protecting the country he loved. He stayed low, crouching through sagebrush and hiding behind rocks until he was at an even higher elevation where no one would fathom looking. A distant ridge was his landmark and his guide to escape.

***

A sudden, muffled blast and flash of light caught Kilbraide's attention. Chaos filled the amphitheater and Kilbraide immediately snapped to his right, searching up the hill. Through his riflescope he saw an outcropping of rocks, and another, and a third outcropping even higher. He saw movement in the brush and an outline going over a ridge. Stevens.

He fired. After that, nothing.

CHAPTER THIRTY-SIX

Stevens balanced his backpack and saw the thick canopy of branches several feet high, woven together. But the late afternoon sun was moving west and he didn't see the rock on the path he was blazing. His foot caught it and he stumbled but regained his balance. Mother Nature's thin branches and thorny brambles were worse than any person he had ever encountered, and they left numerous scratches as he made his way through them.

His legs were weaker, and his muscles burned more than he expected. Soldiering on was something he couldn't do indefinitely. The trip up the mountain that took him away from the Olympic Village forced him to duck behind rocks and crouch near overgrown sage to avoid police helicopters looking for suspicious movements. Hurrying down the opposite side, on a trail used mostly by deer, to the eastern suburbs of Salt Lake City forced him to slow his pace. The slope was difficult and at times treacherous with slippery gravel and loose dirt.

By the time he reached the road at the base of the hills, his thighs were sore from the steep trail and unsteady footing.

A police siren blared so he hit the ground hard, but it passed and he got up. In the distance, Stevens saw the cruiser behind an average-looking sedan. Chaos had probably erupted all over the country after Zach Price's assassination but running stop signs or going too fast in a residential zone still warranted a ticket.

His phone suddenly had a signal and erupted with a continual vibrating. He fumbled for it, took a quick look, and saw numerous missed calls and a stream of text messages from Amanda.

Where are you?

Bob, I'm scared. Did you hear?

This is horrible.

Bob, answer me!

Stevens wanted to answer, but he also wanted out of the area. He dashed over the rough ground to his truck hidden from view in a clump of bushes and small trees. It was covered with a camouflaged tarp, brush, and branches. He yanked back the tarp spewing dust and debris, and opened the driver's side door. He tossed his equipment inside. His stomach growled. Taking a deep breath didn't slow the adrenaline that was still pumping when he grabbed his smartphone and stuck it on the dashboard's phone holder. He started the truck, hit the gas, and made it onto the narrow road, passing the poor guy getting a ticket. He wound through the neighborhood, made his way onto the freeway, and headed south when another text came through.

Flight's ready. Evac.

That meant a private flight out of the country to lounge and regroup—and it meant goodbye to ever seeing Amanda again, sadly unavoidable. Retreating was part of the gig. The more rocks you throw at a hornet's nest, the likelier you are to get stung. Stevens held the wheel with one hand and tried to reply *Ok* with the other. But his arms were as cramped as his legs and a car's horn blared. He swerved out of the lane but caught himself. *Just drive.*

The exit for Highway 242 was several miles ahead and another text hit as he got closer.

Confirm.

"Just wait a goddamn second," Stevens fumed, turning on the headlights to combat the angle of the sun as it moved farther west.

Cars zipped past as he carefully changed lanes and made the exit south of Salt Lake. The area had obligatory gas stations and fast-food brand names on the south and north corners. Hunger hit and stabbed his gut. Getting a burger and fries would help but pulling into a restaurant alongside I-15 was too damned risky. What if cops were crawling around?

The road headed west into the red glow of early evening. Stevens drove into a more residential area away from the interstate. Another text appeared.

OMG! I can't believe it.

Amanda.

It's horrible, Bob. Sickening.

Stevens practically slammed on the brakes and pulled to the curb. He typed *I'm here*, but didn't send it. His flight was waiting and they'd whisk him out of the country and care for all his needs, including women. He deleted his reply.

He pulled the truck out of park and continued on to a solitary eatery on the edge of town with burritos, burgers, fries. *Paradise found.* The interstate was at least two miles behind him.

He ordered in the glow of overhead lights with his head turned to one side in case security cameras were rolling. But from the looks inside the little restaurant, it was likely they had never installed any. A man who looked bored, tired and didn't bother to glance up took his order. The guy had probably never heard of Zach Price and didn't seem like he would care.

Amanda wasn't finished. Another text came through.

I wish you were here. Where are you?

The food arrived and Stevens felt like he had to reply. *No bars. Will call when possible. Don't be scared. Heading back. Driving. Be there in less than eleven.* He took a huge bite out of the hamburger and wondered what he had just committed to.

I need you, she messaged. *I'm a mess. So damned scared. Thanks. Please hurry.*

I will, he replied.

Memories of Amanda's smile and dancing with her lit his thoughts. Stevens finished the burger and grabbed a mouthful of fries when a text from his handlers arrived.

Confirm location. Evacuate now.

The moment gripped him. He couldn't let Amanda down. Screw Black Eagle.

His phone vibrated again.

What do I do, Bob? I'm nervous. Scared. My boss was murdered.

He hated the thought of Amanda worried and in so much pain, but she would thank him later. She was so beautiful when she was happy.

Don't worry. You're safe. I'll look after you. Be there soon.

Amanda texted again. *Promise?*

Promise. Stevens took a deep breath.

Then another text from Black Eagle. *Status. Confirm. Now!*

Stevens had no choice. He'd have to evacuate, or they'd hunt him down and eliminate him. His mind was made up. All he had to do was jump in the truck, drive back to the interstate, and—

Amanda sent more texts. She had lost composure. Her scent played heavily in his mind. Her voice, smile, and innocent eyes along with her kisses and soft-spoken enjoyment of him. Nights in bed with her were rich and the only joy he had known in years.

Then it struck him as he got back into the truck. If he fled the country and left Amanda, then he wasn't a free man. He was answering to someone else who dictated his every move and that ruined the belief in the freedoms he had risked his life for.

He started driving and realized he felt the freest when holding her.

He and Amanda exchanged more text messages and each ended with *I love you* as he headed west.

But Black Eagle wasn't finished. They kept texting. *Status, confirm. Confirm.*

He looked at his phone while he drove the lonely stretch and weighed the consequences again, but his mind was made up. If he didn't answer, they'd never know what happened to him. He knew he needed to get to Amanda quickly, before anybody else, and then they could disappear.

It was over. He was done.

Tired of Black Eagle. Tired of this life.

He rolled down the window and tossed the phone. Amanda's kiss would taste wonderfully sweet.

CHAPTER THIRTY-SEVEN

Ranting university professors blanketed social media with furious rhetoric. Angry up-and-coming techies interviewed on news channels and across the internet were despondent, but they vowed to fight and keep Price's dream of the Free People, Free World Initiative alive.

They hated how Price was killed in public, like an arrogant spectacle, a daring game of *catch me if you can.* Researchers in academia and opinion makers wondered how law enforcement in the twenty-first century failed time and again to nab the bad guy. Protestors were marching and destroying sprawling campuses in Silicon Valley and trashing universities from San Diego to Pittsburgh to Portland, Maine.

Paranoia paralyzed rational thinking and everyone wondered who was the next target. The match was struck and a full-fledged fire was burning out of control. Antifa and BLM were already rioting in cities where police forces were decimated by the Defund the Police movement.

The country was about to explode into chaos. The Left was blaming the Right, and the Right was blaming the Left.

Local law enforcement and the FBI had descended on every building around the Olympic Center, locking down condos and questioning residents. No one was allowed to leave the amphitheater until after dark. A full-scale manhunt started on the hillsides and continued throughout the night, culminating in the discovery of the shooter's hide and the *One Shot, One Kill* patch. This was the connection to the other murders.

Kilbraide and Catalonia were removed from the fervor, reading Amanda Richelieu's text messages. Amanda was blind to Vanguard tapping her phone and how the heartfelt text messages, revealing the depth of her fear and her desire for Bob Stevens, was being dissected, looking for the tiniest of clues.

Amanda had texted and dialed Stevens' number many times. It was strange, though, that Stevens had answered her and then his responses went haywire, as his signal bounced from one part of the country to another.

Catalonia was reading Amanda's messages and it was obvious that anxiety was eating her alive since her boss had just been assassinated on live TV. But then the messages became scrambled and impossible to decipher. Then nothing. The signal dropped.

"We're so fucked," she moaned.

A tech looked up from a nearby screen. "Gone. Nothing. No trace."

Anger boiled inside Kilbraide.

Did Stevens disappear again? Was he shuttled away from the scene?

It wasn't fair. A man on the loose was given orders from some uncontrollable government or quasi-government agency to assassinate specific targets that they deemed were a threat to America. And without question or hesitation, Stevens carried out his mission faithfully.

And that gave Kilbraide an idea. He thought about what he'd seen hidden in Stevens' cabin. Locked away like a treasure. A simple memento, a photo of Stevens and Amanda. He was a trained assassin and not supposed to have feelings, not supposed to get involved. But to keep that picture tucked away, it meant something to him. All the recorded texts and phone calls between Stevens and Amanda ran through Kilbraide's head. It was all out of character for the man—he was in love.

"Fuck, Kilbraide, I can't believe it. You had him. So close. And you missed. That was our best chance yet and now we're starting over. They've already pulled him." said Catalonia. "He got away, again."

"No. Not this time." Kilbraide shook his head.

"What do you mean, 'no?'"

"I mean, he's on a rescue mission." Kilbraide was ready and knew exactly what to do.

CHAPTER THIRTY-EIGHT

Stevens took his foot off the brake and let his truck coast beneath the familiar canopy of trees while he fought to keep his mind clear. He was tired from driving through the night but had arrived a couple of hours before sunrise. Amanda's potential embrace and kisses were tempting but he still needed to be careful. Being overly cautious allowed him to carry out his mission, it was part of his psyche. So was stepping into the unknown. Every assignment was a risk, but he brushed thoughts of danger aside since he was confident in the surveillance that he was trained to do.

Nervousness rattled him now since this was a personal rescue operation, one he hadn't planned on. But whisking Amanda into his life and away from her cabin and a career in tech that was poisoning her is what needed to be done. He loved her too much to let her suffer.

While he crept along the road, the truck hit a rut, shook, and jangled his composure. *Shit.* Stevens felt like he'd been away for a lifetime. He cut the headlights as he inched nearer to Amanda's cabin, navigating with a slight amount of moonlight. He kept a light foot on the gas to stay as stealthy as possible while searching the surrounding areas for any threat. But from who? His own people? Kilbraide? He knew a target was on his back and that he had to make this quick.

There. Her place. A light was on.

He put the gear in neutral and coasted by while scanning her driveway, her car, the dark woods, and the ridge behind. Everything looked ordinary.

Stevens put the truck back in gear, drove slowly at just a few miles per hour until he saw his cabin, as empty as when he left. The driveway was clean, no tire tracks in the dirt. No one had been there. It was as dark as it normally was at night when he turned out the light and fell asleep, tormented by the pain of knowing he could never be with Amanda. Until now.

He drove on, reached the end of the lane, turned around, and struggled to quell his hope. *Steady. Steady.*

But always be cautious. Be on the lookout.

Stevens coasted to a stop in front of Amanda's driveway, using the handbrake so his taillights wouldn't alert anyone watching for his presence. Not that he was scared. Fear had trouble finding him because he was always prepared. Like now. He reached beneath his jacket, grabbed the handgun from the holster to double-check it, slamming the magazine back in before opening the truck door and stepping into the darkness. The thick vegetation gave him cover as he scurried, hiding behind one tree, watching, waiting, and moving to the next. He listened intently, examined the shadows of the woods, and convinced himself no one was there to intercept him as he moved closer to the cabin. A light in the kitchen was still on, but the rest of the house was dark. He took it as a sign that she was able to get to sleep, and that lightened his mood and gave him hope.

His work was finally done. Mission accomplished and never again. He prayed America got the message. Now to take Amanda to a better place and a more wonderful world.

He crept to the bedroom window and could see her silhouette under the covers. Stevens hurried to the front door, quietly rejoicing in his good fortune. And why not? He had always done the right thing. He tapped on the door lightly and waited. He tapped harder, waited, and knocked again. Then Amanda opened the door. There she was, wearing a long T-shirt and robe.

"Bob."

"Shh."

He stepped inside, shut the door behind and held her. The kiss was magical and warmed him completely. But there wasn't any time. The Black Ops, both his and Kilbraide's, would figure out that he'd come here. They had to leave now.

"We've got to go," he said.

"Bob, what's happening—" She ran a hand over his chest. "What's that?"

"A gun."

She looked confused. "Why do you have a gun?"

"For your protection."

"What're you—?"

Stevens cupped a hand over her mouth.

"Don't talk. Just listen and I'll explain. Do you trust me? I mean, really trust me?"

Stevens pressed hard while she thought about her answer with fear lighting up her face. He had been racked with anguish and guilt over what to tell her, how to get her out of here, to run away with him. What would she believe? The truth? No, she wasn't ready for that. He stared into her eyes and lowered his hand from her mouth.

"Why are you acting like this? What's going on?" Amanda sputtered and was defiant. "Why do you have a gun? And don't ever put your hand over my mouth again."

"Look, I'll explain everything on the way, but right now, we need to get out of here."

"Bob, I'm not going anywhere until you tell me what the hell you're talking about." She narrowed her eyes. "Why is your face so scratched up?"

Stevens took a deep breath, trying to get the half-truth, no, the lie, straight in his head. "Amanda, everything you know about me is the truth, except I'm not a financial planner. Not anymore. I work undercover for the government. It's a long story, but—"

"What? Like the FBI or something?"

"Something. Listen. We've been involved in tracking the recent assassinations and trying to plot their next moves."

Amanda tried to process what Stevens was saying, but it sounded too strange. "Are you crazy? This is like something out of some spy movie, Bob."

"Listen to me. We've come across information that shows the killer's next targets may be more execs at Zudder."

"What?" Amanda ran a hand through her hair. "Why? Oh, my God. Am I a target? Am I in danger?"

"Maybe. I'm not trying to scare you, but—"

Her knees went weak and Stevens tried to hold her. But she stepped back in fear, unsure.

"Don't. Am I in danger from you?"

Hurt coursed through his body. It wasn't the reaction he expected.

"Amanda, no. I'm trying to protect you. Just in case. That's why we need to leave. Immediately! Pack a bag, only what you need. Quickly. I'll get us somewhere safe. I promise. I'll explain everything."

"I don't know. I can't think right now. Explain!"

"I will. Trust me. We have to go now. Hurry."

Confusion swept across Amanda's face. She had a decision to make and didn't know what to do. She stared at Stevens. His eyes were pleading, full of worry, love. She made up her mind, turned, and dashed into the bedroom while Stevens glanced out the windows. He grabbed fruit and vegetables from the refrigerator, stuffed them in a bag, and met Amanda at the front door where she fought back tears and clutched an overnight bag.

"Trust me," he said. "I love you."

"I love you, too." Her voice was quivering, unsure.

"Ready?"

"No. But—"

He interrupted her with a firm tone. "We have to go. Now."

Stevens opened the door, grabbed the bags, and led the way down the dark driveway to his truck while Amanda locked, shut the door behind her, and hurried to join him. He threw the bags in the back and they climbed inside.

"Just tell me what's happening," she said.

"I will." He started up and turned the truck. "I need to stop by my place, grab some things, and we'll be on our way."

Amanda's voice quivered. "Is someone really after me?"

"Yes." He pulled into his driveway, slowed to a stop, and turned to her. "I'll be quick. Wait here."

Amanda sighed with worry crawling in her eyes.

Stevens slipped out of the truck and glanced side to side as he rushed to the cabin, searching the perimeter. Nothing. Going to the back door, he inserted the key, unlocked it, and snuck inside, using what little ambient light there was.

A sensation caught Stevens' attention, like a presence in the house. He stopped, listened, but heard nothing and continued.

In the bedroom, he pulled together a bag of clothes, some survival gear and weapons from various hidden caches, and then, the most important items. He opened the trapdoor, reached inside, and grabbed the photo of him and Amanda—then the photo of him and his wife and a letter she had written. She had addressed it to him shortly before she died from an overdose, expressing her love and encouraging him to be strong. He stuffed everything inside his bag. He needed to hurry. Black Ops would be here soon.

It was time to move on. He was with Amanda now and he knew the route to drive out of California, into Nevada, and up to his cabin in Montana. His handlers didn't even know about that place. Nobody did. Bugging out to the backwoods never seemed so inviting.

A sensation settled over him again. Stronger. He couldn't dismiss it. Stevens took out his gun, stepped into the kitchen, and froze. His blood turned to ice when he saw a ghostly silhouette staring at him.

The kitchen light clicked on.

"Hi Bob." Kilbraide was sitting on the counter and had flicked the switch.

Stevens blinked as his eyes adjusted and saw Kilbraide with his handgun at the ready.

"Forget your beer?" Kilbraide grabbed a bottle from off the counter, took a swig, and set it down.

CHAPTER THIRTY-NINE

Like two cowboys in the old west facing off at high noon, the men kept their guns trained on each other, both wary of making a sudden move.

"Clever." Stevens stood with his legs shoulder-width, showing confidence. "Very good."

"Thanks. I was here once before but, unfortunately, you weren't home. So, I figured you'd be back."

Stevens craned his neck and looked at a broken window. "Did you do that?"

"Yeah. Sorry."

Stevens looked at his gun and then Kilbraide's weapon. "This is awkward. Tough to talk while holding these."

"Guess so. Shows there's a lack of trust." Kilbraide kept his gaze steady. "You want to talk?"

"I have. For some time."

"About what?"

"Patriots. You and me."

Kilbraide furrowed a brow like he was thinking about it. "Patriots?"

"Standing for what's right, like freedom."

"What freedoms?" Kilbraide remained steady. "Like life, liberty, and the pursuit of happiness? Freedom of speech, maybe?"

"Yeah, exactly." Stevens agreed. "Protecting our Constitution, and our freedoms from tyranny and the bullshit that's going on."

"Hmm." Kilbraide scrunched his face. "Don't you think you've been acting like a tyrant?"

"I've been acting for the good of America."

"By killing people when they're expressing their right to free speech?"

"I don't just go around killing people," said Stevens. "It's sanctioned."

"By who? Some mysterious Black Ops that sends you a text? You don't even know who you're working for. Do you?"

"I follow orders."

"To kill American civilians?" countered Kilbraide.

"I take out those who—"

"Even if that's against your oath? What about those you killed in LA?"

Stevens paused to hold his emotions in check. "That's different. They killed my wife."

Kilbraide sounded empathetic. "You mean when she overdosed?"

"Yeah."

"She got tangled up in drugs, Bob. Nobody forced her. Sadly, she did that to herself."

"Which wouldn't have happened if people weren't profiting from them."

"What did Julius Brae do to you? Zach Price, or Martha Schallum. Or that asshole senator from the Bay Area?"

"Come on Kilbraide, you were a Ranger. Use what little brains you have," said Stevens.

"Humor me."

Both men relaxed their stances.

"Brae and Price, two peas in a pod," said Stevens. "Rich, arrogant, and yeah, geniuses in their own right. I can't deny them that. But controlling information, only letting people use their platforms if it aligns with their radical leftist points of view, banning those that they disagree with. It's not right, it's un-American. For Christ's sake Kilbraide, they de-platformed a sitting U.S. president and altered the course of an election. They needed to be held accountable. And Senator Alanasian, he was a real piece of crap, rotten to the *corps*. And yeah, I mean *Marine corps*. Always undercutting National security, and lining his own pockets. Lying to Congress and in bed with Brae and Price. Yeah, who was the chairman of the committee that brought them before Congress for censoring free speech? Alanasian. Did anything happen? Were they shut down or fined? No. And all of this goes over the airwaves through the mainstream media, the fake news. And who's the number one fake news mouthpiece? Schallum. Spewing her lying rhetoric day after day to every brainwashed lefty, who in turn, votes for assholes like Alanasian, who supports Price and Brae. It's all rigged to bring down our country and turn us into a socialist utopia with their Free People, Free World Initiative. Such propagandist bullshit. Nothing but smoke and mirrors to brainwash the—"

Stevens stopped and took a breath to settle.

Kilbraide gave him a moment to cool down. "Conspiracy theory, much? Are you even listening to what you're saying?"

"I'm speaking the truth."

"The truth as you see it. Look, I don't agree with their views and methods, not at all. But they too, have a right to their beliefs. And just like you, I took an oath to defend—"

Stevens interrupted. "—defend the Constitution against all enemies, foreign and domestic… and if you remember the rest of it, it says to follow orders of officers above me. Well, I'm doing both, following orders and protecting against domestic threats. They're the enemy, not me. Why can't you see that?"

"Because you took away their constitutional rights, and you took away their lives. You murdered them. And now, here we are. And you already know what my orders are." Kilbraide raised his gun again.

"I do. I'm disappointed, really." Stevens raised his.

"Yeah, why?"

Stevens studied Kilbraide carefully. "You have a talent that almost matches mine." He smiled.

"And your point?

"You won the last round in LA, and I just wanted a chance to even the score. See how good you really are. Play a little friendly game of HOG."

"Hunter of Gunman," Kilbraide responded. "Is that why you wrote my name on your patches?"

"That's right. I knew they'd send someone after me, and I wanted to go up against the best. Well, second best. So, I volunteered you."

"Well, I'm not going to say 'Thank you,' and I certainly can't say that I enjoyed this very much, but here I am."

"And yes, because you missed me, here we are," Stevens agreed. "To be honest, there's no retirement from Black Eagle. Once you're in, you're in and there's no way out. They would eventually have sent someone to disappear me, but I wasn't going to let that happen. I wanted to go out on my own terms. So that's where you come in."

"You wanted me to kill you?"

"Yeah, but this isn't exactly like I pictured it, so what do we do now?"

"You know my answer," says Kilbraide. "But go ahead. You tell me."

"Deep inside I've been doing a lot of soul-searching, and I think I'm done. I just want to lead a normal life, settle down, raise a family, get a dog and a cat, and let the world turn without me."

"Yeah, the American dream."

"That's what I'm going to be doing, Kilbraide. Re-group, focus." Stevens was adamant. "And that's what I desperately want to talk to you about. What I've been doing. Isn't that for a better America? Isn't that what you want, too? To raise our kids in the America we grew up in?"

"It is, Bob. A land where the laws are respected and upheld and it's through those laws that justice is served."

Stevens glanced at his weapon. "It's hard to talk when we're pointing these at each other."

"True. Why don't you put yours down?"

Stevens felt encouraged. "I'd love to, Kilbraide. I really do want to have our own little beer summit."

"Then put your gun down."

For a split second, the thought made sense and Stevens lowered his arm a fraction of an inch. But he stopped. "After you."

"Too bad there's such a lack of trust, isn't there?" Kilbraide looked concerned.

"Yeah, look at us. Both working for a rival Black Ops. Shared service to our country. We got a lot in common, Kilbraide."

"You think so?"

"Absolutely." Stevens eyed him closely. "Let me get some things, just some food, and I'll be out of here, but we can continue talking. I got your number."

Kilbraide kept his gun steady.

Stevens sighed, annoyed. "Come on, Kilbraide. There's a reason you haven't killed me yet." He could step back, take a chance, and run out the front. "Say something."

"I've already said it. Put your weapon down and we can talk."

"Cut the shit." Stevens slid his finger to the trigger. "Work with me here."

"I'm serious, Bob."

"We both know that you don't want to kill me. And I don't want to kill you. We're brothers. I want a new start, I want a new life, and you can give me that. I'll walk out slowly. Let me go. You can say you got here too late. I was already gone. No one will ever know."

"I can't do that. Put the gun down."

"And I can't do that."

"We have a problem then."

"Kilbraide, goddamn it."

"Do it, Bob."

"Okay. You don't want to talk. You don't want to work this out. Now what? You're going to have to shoot me and I don't think you will." Stevens felt a chill. "So, I'm just going to—" Stevens moved one foot toward the door.

"Don't!" Kilbraide stayed steady and kept his eyes locked on Stevens.

"You think it has to be me or you? Is that what you're thinking?" Stevens sounded hurt.

"I've told you what to do," said Kilbraide.

Stevens was bewildered. "What do you care, where I go? I've done my part, I followed orders, I've served my country. Now, I've got a life to live. And a beautiful woman to live it with." Stevens was annoyed at the standoff. "Just let me walk out. It's simple. Who's going to know?"

"I'll know."

"That's deep. So, you think by bringing me in that justice will be served? You know as well as I do that I'll never see the inside of a cell or make it into a courtroom." Stevens pleaded. "Fuck it, Kilbraide. Give me a fresh start with Amanda."

"Give it up, Bob. Put your gun down. It's over."

"Goddamn it, Kilbraide."

Silence fell until the *Click*. A normally quiet sound that was amplified hundreds of times louder in each man's mind. A burst of gunfire followed.

Kilbraide pulled the trigger, leaping off the counter and grimacing from a vicious bullet tearing into his shoulder while Bob Stevens crumpled to the floor, twisting onto his back with blood spilling from his chest.

Both men had reacted to the click that came from the front door where Amanda had entered…and now stood screaming as Bob Stevens lay dying.

CHAPTER FORTY

Headaches were invisible but they were real and Kilbraide was feeling every part of his brain on fire as morning light slipped through the blinds he forgot to close. His wheels were turning harder and harder trying to figure out—what? Amanda? Stevens? The Black Ops running this country?

What the hell?

He sighed. Though it was early morning, a beer and Vicodin sounded more appealing than breakfast.

Kilbraide was still in the early years of his career as a detective, but he had met many families who suffered loss of property or loss of loved ones. His heart couldn't break too deeply for them because there was always another case to be solved. Building a wall around your emotions and numbing yourself came with the territory.

Maybe that's why Amanda's grief troubled him so much. He had seen her collapse in shock and listened to her agony as Catalonia's team whisked her into a witness protection program, a new life she didn't ask for and had no choice in. He felt badly for her. And through no fault of her own, the idyllic world she had created for herself was gone and she could no longer exist in it. She'd be listed as a missing person and in time would just be a memory in the minds of her friends and family. So many lives ruined. Sad. Another casualty of Stevens.

Amanda would never leave his thoughts completely, but the power of her sobs would diminish when he got himself wrapped back up in work around Los Angeles. If he decided to stay. Or maybe he should just disappear for a while as well. Nothing was certain any longer.

His thoughts drifted back to Stevens. He felt sorry for him. He was a true patriot and decorated Marine who had served his country proudly, but after the death of his wife he changed. He was broken, twisted, his views were warped, and he got caught up in something beyond his control. The way it ended was the only possible outcome. His service, his life, and his existence – wiped from history. Sad.

Kilbraide got out of bed in his boxers, wincing with his shoulder on the mend. Steven's bullet ripped through his chest muscle, leaving a good-sized hole, but luckily it missed vital organs, arteries, and bones. Surgery, a few days in the hospital, and now he was finally back home living on the fourth floor of a Hollywood apartment building. He found his way to the bathroom and thought it fitting that he lived just below the Hollywood sign. It was a town where people labored to turn make-believe into their version of reality, just like Catalonia and Vanguard did. And still he had no real answers. Who did he just put his life on the line for? Who are they? Who do they answer to? What's their agenda? And what side of history will they go down on? Lots of questions, but no answers.

Opening the medicine cabinet and the bottle of Motrin he found was awkward with his right arm in a sling. Motrin! What the hell? Doesn't do a thing for the type of pain he was in. He needed a real pain killer, something to help him be numb in mind and body, like Vicodin or codeine. Hell, he'd even go for a shot of morphine right now just to take the edge off. But in the eyes of the government, you're an addict if you want something more than aspirin for pain.

He swallowed the Motrin. His headache subsided a bit as he sat on his easy chair and scrolled through his phone trying to catch up on sports scores. He came across a stunning news story. *Fugitive assassin cornered, turns gun on himself.*

Unbelievable.

The story was released late in a busy news cycle, just as another made-up news story being fed to the masses was about to distract the public from whatever else was going on—all of it perfectly planned out and timed to sway opinion one way or another.

Kilbraide read it anyway and after drudging through the reporting about white supremacy and banning guns he found a couple sentences describing how the Federal authorities closed in on the suspected sniper in Idaho. After a brief stand-off, they found the man dead inside his cabin with a self-inflicted bullet wound to the head.

Officials went on to say that he acted alone in killing the leading minds in tech, politics, and media. They painted a cliché picture of him saying that he was a prepper, a gun nut, and a self-radicalized loner living off the grid with no known associates, family, or friends. And of course, they stated that he had a *manifesto*, they always use that term, but gave no details on the writings. The article ended stating that there was no further threat to the public and the authorities were confident that the case was closed.

One photo accompanied the article. It was a grainy image of a small cabin tucked into the side of a hill and camouflaged with brush and dirt. Through the open door lay a body, blurred out, so as not to offend anyone.

Kilbraide wondered who the poor scapegoat was.

A drug addict? A homeless guy? Somebody from a rival Black Ops? Hell, probably nobody at all. It's all smoke, mirrors, and photoshop anyway.

Kilbraide sighed, tossed his phone on the coffee table and he probably would've punched his hand through the wall if his arm hadn't been healing. *All bullshit.* One obscure government operation fighting another and he had been pulled in to do the dirty work.

It was a dangerous game to play, but Kilbraide spun the proverbial dice in his thoughts while he stumbled about the kitchen trying to brew a lousy cup of coffee.

What if he called every news outlet in LA and told them where he'd been?

What if he wrote a book and contacted every podcaster on the planet?

What if…?

It wasn't worth it. Nobody, except conspiracy theorists, would believe him. He'd be mocked and labeled as a nut-job, or worse, he'd get "disappeared."

His stomach was growling, demanding something meaty and rich like an omelet and sausages with a mug of strong, hair-raising coffee. No way would he fix it himself. Time to get out to his favorite diner down the street. Making it to the bedroom, he was struggling to put on some jeans and a T-shirt when he heard the annoying buzz of his cell on the coffee table.

Kilbraide hustled into the other room and picked it up. "Yeah?"

"You sound like you're still on the trail."

It was Detective Tom Stone. A voice as welcomed as fresh air on a smoggy LA day.

"Stone? Damn nice hearing from you."

"I hoped you'd think so. Hey, I was just watching the news. Every channel is running the same *B.S.* Not even the top story, amazing. Can't wait to hear your version of what really happened. Unofficially and off the record, of course."

Kilbraide hesitated. "Of course."

"But there's time for that later," said Stone. "How about some breakfast?"

"Yeah. Your timing's perfect. I was just thinking about it."

"Great. Jake and I are on the way. We'll be there in ten."

"Looking forward to it."

Kilbraide hung up, headed back into his bedroom, and glanced out the window at the gray marine layer that'd soon burn off with the

California sun. His phone rang again. A number he didn't recognize so he let it go.

But it rang once more, stopped, and rang again. He answered. "Kilbraide."

"Kilbraide?"

"Yeah. I just said it was."

"Catalonia."

"I can tell by your sweet disposition. What's up?" It was natural to have a bad feeling in the pit of his stomach whenever he heard her voice.

"How's your shoulder?"

"Still attached."

Catalonia was matter of fact. "I see you've not lost your funny bone."

"Still got it," said Kilbraide.

"Good to know."

He was tempted to ask if she'd ever found her heart but decided against it and waited through the silence for her to continue.

"Got something to ask you."

Kilbraide struggled to put on and tie his running shoes. "No, I'm not ready to get married."

"I'm sure you'll find the right one someday but that's not what I was asking. Wondering if you really want to settle back into your dull routine?"

"You mean the boredom of identifying bloated bodies and tracking killers while occasionally bumping into celebrities? That kind of dull routine?"

"Something like that."

Kilbraide couldn't wait to hang up. "I'll give it a try for a while."

"Okay. Suit yourself."

"Wait. Why?"

He listened carefully and imagined Catalonia's lips parting into a devious smile.

"Just wondering. I might have a need for someone like you. That's all."

There was always a need. "You really like your job; you excel in it and find some twisted pleasure in what you do, don't you?" asked Kilbraide.

"I do."

"And I like mine. Listen, I got to get on with things here, but thanks for calling."

"Glad I did," said Catalonia. "Okay. Goodbye, then."

"Bye."

The line went dead. He turned out the light, locked the door, and walked down four flights of stairs to wait for Stone and Jake. Kilbraide smiled as the familiar Crown Vic pulled to the curb and he climbed in the back. Greetings were exchanged and it felt good to be with friends as they drove to breakfast. Conversation faded into white noise as he stared out the window in deep thought. So clever of Catalonia not to say anything directly about her *need*, but it was obvious, he knew what it was. She planted the seed, damn her, and now he was thinking about it.

AUTHORS' NOTE:

We're passionate about creating memorable characters and hope you've felt the passion on this adventure.

Your reviews help us reach more readers so please leave one on Amazon, Facebook, Goodreads and other outlets.

"Fast-paced page turners with suspense that starts at the beginning and keeps building right to the end."

Sign up for our Tom Stone Detective Stories Newsletter for sneak previews and discounts.

Find us online:

Facebook: www.facebook.com/tomstonedetectivestories/

Blog: www.tomstonedetectiveblog.wordpress.com/

Website: www.carvedinstone.media/tomstonedetectivestories/

Email: dettomstonestories@gmail.com

***

READER REVIEWS

A Nitty Gritty Christmas

"Enormously engaging and captivating. Read the book. You won't regret it."

"I am a sucker for suspense and this was loaded with it. I really got into the well-developed characters. Looking forward to the next one! By the way, would make a killer movie!"

"'Nitty Gritty' is a brilliant way to describe it. I felt like I was stepping into the Los Angeles underbelly and living the life of an L.A. police detective."

Sweltering Summer Nights

"The story is realistic, brings about the relevant drug issues and social inequalities that comes with it. Tom Stone is a well-rounded man, one hell of a detective with a big heart. Strong family values such as love and compassion despite the non-traditional family setup."

"I loved the LA Medical Dispensary concept. Tom Stone is quiet a perceptive and intuitive detective with a great partner Jake. Angelino brought a touch of Tony Montana, from Scarface as the villain"

"Great action thriller! A gripping story of police work and urban life. The plot is intriguing and kept us in the book. Highly recommend!"

Day of the Dead

"Drugs, violence, women all play a part and with Halloween fast approaching things are starting to get messy. This is a fast-paced page turner with suspense that starts at the beginning and keeps building right to the end. Action all the way through it is a great read."

"I enjoyed reading this story! Don and Lon kept the pace moving. It was quick read, I felt comfortable with the characters and places in the book. I recommend 'Day of the Dead' to all looking for a quick detective story!"

"This book had a great pace and it took me straight off on a brilliant ride to the fantastic ending! I was hooked right from the beginning and I read it in a few hours as I didn't want to put the book down."

One Shot, One Kill

"Gripping. A study in what drives a killer into madness. It was an edge of the seat page turner. I couldn't put it down, and I can't wait till the next in the series."

"I like the way Stone and his friends interact with each other, like a family, bringing community to the otherwise fractured city of Los Angeles."

"The story launches with and intense beginning and keeps a suspenseful pace that leads to a surprise ending."

Subterfuge

"I liked the pacing, and the mystery of the characters."

"The authors keep the story real by including Tom Stone and Jake's personal life with their friends and family."

"It's a page turner! I thought it would take me a couple of weeks to read it, but even watching our grandson for 5 days, I finished the book in a week. Well done!"

A Deadly Path

"The BEST little story I've read in a long time. If you haven't read any of the other Tom Stone Detective Stories start with this one. It'll intrigued you... I loved it."

"4 Stars for 'A Deadly Path.' Action fills the pages; a father's frustration swiftly turns into protectiveness and sacrifice; and a series of murders in the city comes to a chilling conclusion. 'A Deadly Path' is filled with thorny family dynamics and hair-raising suspense."

"A realistic look at a dad, Detective Jake Sharpe, trying to bond with a son he doesn't understand while they're on a hike. A serial killer lies in wait to shoot them and in the tragedy that ensues, Jake is proud of how his son responds. A quick read that celebrates family and justice."

The Smoke Shop Shootout

"Gripping Action and Gut-Wrenching Reality."

"Life on the streets is tough and Smoke Shop Shootout captures some of that grittiness in a thrilling and realistic way. It's a fast read with realistic characters."

"The authors did a good job capturing a strained relationship between a parent and a troubled foster son. It's an emotional story with a message—actions have deadly consequences. It's worth a read."

Massage and Murder

"A thrilling short story that stays with you."

"What is right or a By-the-Book approach to policing? This quick read deals with some of the issues that cops have to deal with every day. It was enjoyable."

"The story is well-written and shows the hardships and decisions that some single mothers have to endure. The characters are true to life, and sometimes life sucks. Events spiral out of control and Stone has to make a tough decision."

Kill Shot

"Pacing is fast, characters are human, with real and believable emotions and thoughts."

"I just finished reading the book and it was great!!!! Seriously. I couldn't stop till I finished it. Kill Shot is a must read. I highly recommend."

"Simkovich and Bixby give Detective Kilbraide his own series with this spin-off of the Tom Stone Detective Stories. It's a great read with well-developed characters. I felt like I knew them personally. And I cannot wait until the next Kilbraide thriller comes out."

***

TOM STONE DETECTIVE STORIES

Tom Stone: A Nitty Gritty Christmas (Novella – Book 1)

Cocaine stuffed into candy bars are appearing throughout Los Angeles. A child's overdose at Christmas pulls Detective Tom Stone and his partner Jake Sharpe into the seedy, underground world of drug smuggling. The duo races to stop whoever's responsible before another innocent life is lost. They piece together clues and close in on the criminals until Stone finds himself trapped, facing certain death at the very hands of the men he was hunting.

Tom Stone: Sweltering Summer Nights (Book 2)

Two murders and a cocaine trail threaten dreams of riches for Anthony Angelino, owner of the High Tide marijuana dispensary in East Hollywood.

Once arrested by Detective Tom Stone on suspicion of smuggling cocaine, the courts set Angelino free and offer a second chance. But the drug cartel that he tried to double cross has a different idea, and when Stone's high school-age daughter is found browsing in the High Tide, Stone starts tracking Angelino and uncovers the ruthlessness of betrayal.

As Stone fights for justice and confronts Angelino's attorney, he finds himself enamored with her strength and beauty—and admires her principles of right and wrong.

Healing his fractured family and keeping Los Angeles safe makes for a long, hot summer.

Tom Stone: Day of the Dead (Book 3)

Multiple murders with one grisly connection have Detectives Tom Stone and Jake Sharpe pursuing every lead. Their main suspect, Anthony Angelino, fresh out of prison, dreams of building a new empire, but his past quickly catches up to him and once again he is on the run from the police, and the drug cartel that tried to ruin him.

The head of the cartel, Frank DeVito, using his vast resources puts a tail on Stone hoping the Detective's investigation will flush out Angelino. Then he can exact his revenge and claim what he says Angelino has stolen – a large shipment of pure cocaine.

Angelino's girlfriend, Sara, caught between right and wrong, pleads for him to escape the deadly lifestyle. As the body count rises, Stone, grappling with his own questions and answers, confronts the challenges in his relationship with Alisha Davidson, Angelino's defense attorney.

Tom Stone: One Shot, One Kill (Book 4)

A vigilante sniper terrorizes Los Angeles with perfectly-timed assassinations, picking off the ultra-wealthy who finance the flow of drugs into the city. As each one falls, a power vacuum is created and a ruthless drug cartel moves in, seeking control of the streets through intimidation, mutilation, and brutally murdering anybody who gets in their way.

Detective Tom Stone and his partner Jake Sharpe suspect mob boss Frank DeVito has a role to play in the carnage after the cartel's shot-caller, a woman in prison named Lil' Jo, orders an assault on DeVito's estate.

Gang violence escalates while the sniper extracts his revenge, eliminating the elite one shot at a time. Stone turns to a new detective on the force, Brian Kilbraide, who had served as a sniper with the Army Rangers.

Stone and his team must race to stop the bloodshed and bring DeVito to justice before the sniper's powerful bullet cuts him dead.

Tom Stone: Subterfuge (Book 5)

A wounded man, fiberglass wreckage, and mysterious blue barrels wash up on a secluded Malibu beach.

Detective Tom Stone jumps into action in this gripping thriller novel and uncovers human trafficking as drug smugglers try a new trick.

The Ojos Negros cartel is back and bolder than ever, forming an uneasy alliance with LA mob boss Frank DeVito. Using hidden sea caves as drop-off points, the new syndicate maneuvers to expand their brutal drug empire, and guns down anyone who stands in their way.

Stone and his team trail the lone survivor, Luis Delgado, who longs to return home to Mexico but is trapped in a deadly game of subterfuge. He vows revenge on the evil men who have destroyed his life and countless others with their greed.

The Detectives race to find Delgado and bring down the cartel, before another innocent victim is killed.

Uncover narco-subs plying the seas with page-turning action—and hold on for an explosive ending.

Tom Stone: A Deadly Path (Short Story)

Detective Jake Sharpe pulls his son Darrell away from video games and joins Tom Stone and the boy he's befriended, Andrew, on a hike in the foothills above Los Angeles. A father and son jaunt becomes a fight for survival when they take a wrong turn on a little-used path.

An armed homeless man with a link to an unsolved cold-case murder is camping in a secluded ravine, and without warning opens fire on them.

Stone and his group have to outwit and outmaneuver his shots in this deadly action-filled short story.

Tom Stone: The Smoke Shop Shootout (Short Story)

'Tis the Season… for a Christmas Crime Thriller Short Story.

A late-night shootout erupts over stolen cigarettes and leaves a Good Samaritan wondering, "Did I do the right thing?"

JoJo is a repeat offender who grew up in foster care. His sister was adopted by a man named Davey, his only connection to family life. When JoJo is released after a short stint in county jail, Davey agrees to pick him up and drive him to a motel near his home.

But when JoJo asks to stop for cigarettes, Davey's in for the fight of his life.

JoJo swipes a pack of smokes causing a fast-moving chain of events that spiral out of control until Detective Tom Stone takes action.

Tom Stone: Massage and Murder (Short Story)

A bloody confrontation at a massage parlor leaves a customer fighting for his life as a masseuse flees into the night.

Detective Tom Stone swings into action, searching for the suspect while monitoring reports on the victim's condition. He investigates a nearby bar where the owner, Jasmine, is closing for the night and wants nothing to do with the police.

A shadowy figure huddles at a back table and Stone approaches to question her, but she escapes to the back parking lot and takes off in her car.

Jasmine, fearful of the power that law enforcement wields, offers to show Stone where the woman lives. She directs him to a run-down motel near a homeless encampment and asks Stone to wait while she heads in first.

Finally, the women lets Stone enter. He questions the suspect, excuses himself to consider the details, and has to face the true meaning of justice.

***

BRIAN KILBRAIDE THRILLERS

Kill Shot: A Brian Kilbraide Thriller

A leading tech guru is the first—shot dead in public.

A popular senator is brutally ambushed during lunchtime.

A sniper's surgical assassinations threaten to rip the country apart.

Bob Stevens, a world-class sniper trained to kill by the military, is using his skills to eliminate the powerful elite who he believes are destroying the America he loves. After each kill, he leaves his calling card—a patch with the name of Detective Brian Kilbraide scrawled across it.

A government Black Ops reinstates Kilbraide's military commission and orders him to track down Stevens and take him out before he can strike again.

Kilbraide is forced into a deadly game of HOG, hunter of gunman, and discovers along the way the disturbing depths of the Shadow Government running the country.

Stevens focuses on his mission, assassinating one public figure after another, but he doesn't count on falling in love with a woman who works for his next target.

Kilbraide closes in.

Time is running out as a thrilling chase ensues across the country.

***

ABOUT THE AUTHORS

Don Simkovich – Don would like to give a shout-out to his wife, Cindy, for her support during the writing process. Storytelling has been part of Don's life and career as a journalist, author, and ghostwriter of blogs and books.

Fiction grabbed his interest at an early age and he has returned to the craft in the past several years, enjoying the mishaps, emotions, and happy endings his characters experience.

He lives with his family and dogs in Pasadena, California.

www.donsimkovich.com
Twitter: @donsimko
Facebook: www.facebook.com/don.simkovich
Instagram: @donsimkovich
Amazon Author Page: www.amazon.com/author/donsimkovich/
Medium: @donsimko
BookBub: Don Simkovich

***

Lon Casler Bixby – Lon is a published author in various genres: Fiction, Poetry, Humor, Photography, and Comic Books. He is also a professional award-winning photographer whose work has been featured in a wide variety of magazines, art & coffee table books, and has also been displayed in Art Galleries throughout the world.

Lon lives out of his photography studio in Burbank, California where he shares his living space with his wonderful, albeit spoiled, Silver Lab named Silver.

Twitter: @LonBixby
Facebook: www.facebook.com/lon.bixby
Instagram: @neoichi
Amazon Author Page: www.amazon.com/author/loncaslerbixby/
Medium: @loncaslerbixby
BookBub: Lon Casler Bixby
Portfolio: www.neoichi.com
Portfolio: www.whileyouweresleeping.photography

***

ABOUT THE COVER ARTIST

Benjamin Southgate – Living beside the Norfolk Broads in England and attending Norwich University of the Arts for a Bachelors in Games Art and Design, specializing in Concept Art; Ben is best known for his talent of visualizing and bringing life to ideas in fully crafted and detailed artwork.

Ben's favorite artist is 18th century French artist Claude-Joseph Vernet, taking awe in the compositional proficiency his pieces display and the diverse moods that his paintings inspire. Ben couples this with his favorite modern day artist Feng Zhu for his creative concepts and techniques.

During leisure Ben enjoys walks in nature, finding comfort in the countryside and capturing the surrounding beauty in photography to assist his craft.

As a freelance artist, he utilizes Photoshop alongside traditional mediums to create character and environment illustrations straight from concept to realization.

You can contact him and view more of his work on his webpage:

www.artstation.com/benjaminsouthgate

***

Made in the USA
Las Vegas, NV
26 November 2022

Made in the USA
Las Vegas, NV
26 November 2022